BABYMOUSE AND FRIENDS*

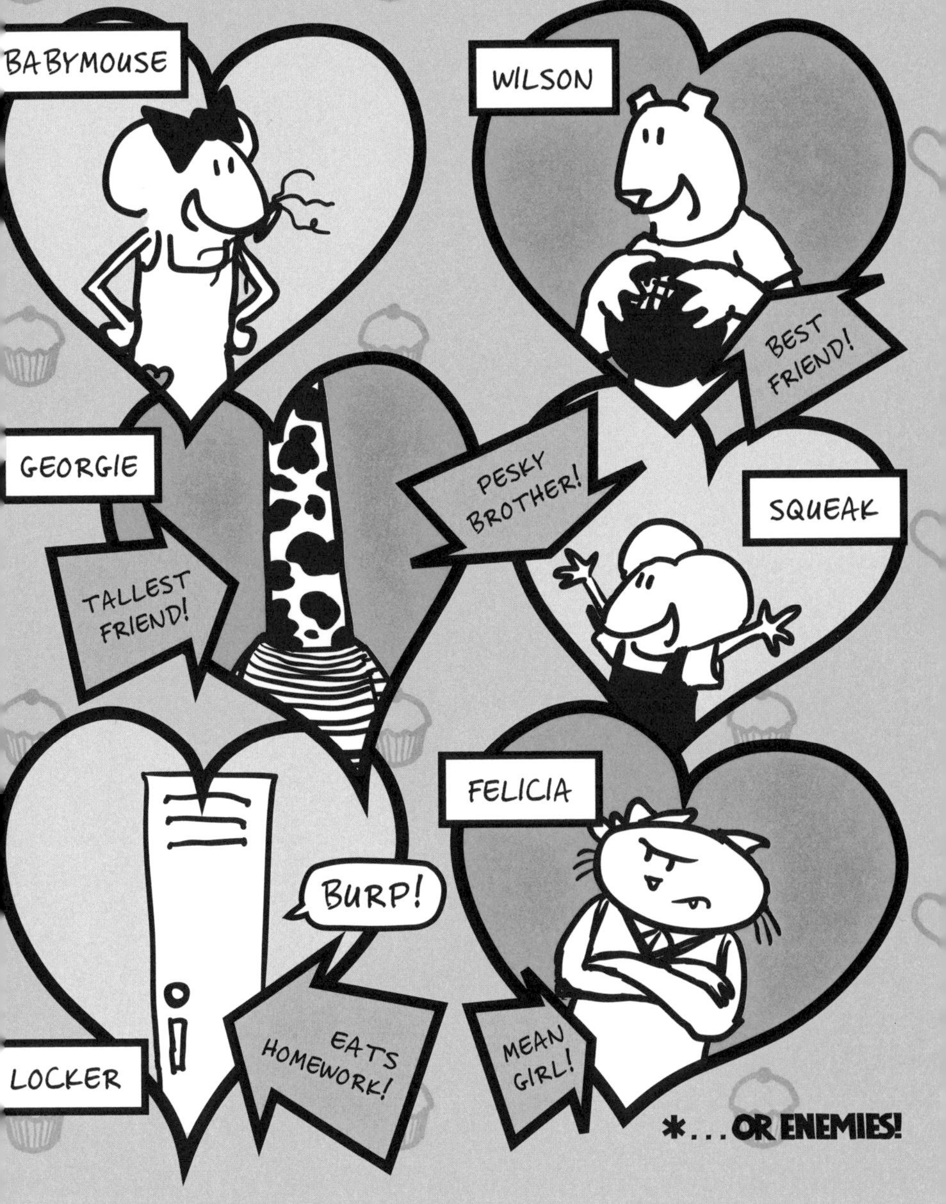
BABYMOUSE
WILSON
BEST FRIEND!
GEORGIE
TALLEST FRIEND!
PESKY BROTHER!
SQUEAK
FELICIA
BURP!
LOCKER
EATS HOMEWORK!
MEAN GIRL!

*. . . OR ENEMIES!

THEY MAKE GREAT BEDTIME STORIES!

BE SURE TO READ **ALL** THE **BABYMOUSE** BOOKS:

#1 BABYMOUSE: Queen of the World!
#2 BABYMOUSE: Our Hero
#3 BABYMOUSE: Beach Babe
#4 BABYMOUSE: Rock Star
#5 BABYMOUSE: Heartbreaker
#6 CAMP BABYMOUSE
#7 BABYMOUSE: Skater Girl
#8 BABYMOUSE: Puppy Love
#9 BABYMOUSE: Monster Mash
#10 BABYMOUSE: The Musical
#11 BABYMOUSE: Dragonslayer
#12 BABYMOUSE: Burns Rubber
#13 BABYMOUSE: Cupcake Tycoon
#14 BABYMOUSE: Mad Scientist
#15 A Very BABYMOUSE Christmas
#16 BABYMOUSE for President
#17 Extreme BABYMOUSE
#18 Happy Birthday, BABYMOUSE
#19 BABYMOUSE: Bad Babysitter

BABYMOUSE
BAD BABYSITTER

BY JENNIFER L. HOLM & MATTHEW HOLM

RANDOM HOUSE 🏠 NEW YORK

ZZZZZZ . . .

All rights reserved. Published in the United States by Random House Children's Books, a division of Random House LLC, a Penguin Random House Company, New York.

Visit us on the Web!
randomhousekids.com
Babymouse.com

Educators and librarians, for a variety of teaching tools, visit us at
RHTeachersLibrarians.com

Library of Congress Cataloging-in-Publication Data
Holm, Jennifer L.
Babymouse : bad babysitter / Jennifer L. Holm and Matthew Holm.—First edition.
   p.   cm.
Summary: "Babymouse discovers that babysitting is not as easy as it sounds."—Provided by publisher
ISBN 978-0-307-93162-7 (trade pbk.)—ISBN 978-0-375-97098-6 (lib. bdg.)—ISBN 978-0-307-97545-4 (ebook)
1. Graphic novels. [1. Graphic novels. 2. Babysitters—Fiction. 3. Moneymaking projects—Fiction.
4. Mice—Fiction. 5. Animals—Fiction. 6. Humorous stories.]
I. Holm, Matthew. II. Title. III. Title: Bad babysitter.
PZ7.7.H65Bacn 2015 741.5'973—dc23 2013047977

MANUFACTURED IN MALAYSIA   10 9 8 7 6 5 4 3 2 1   First Edition

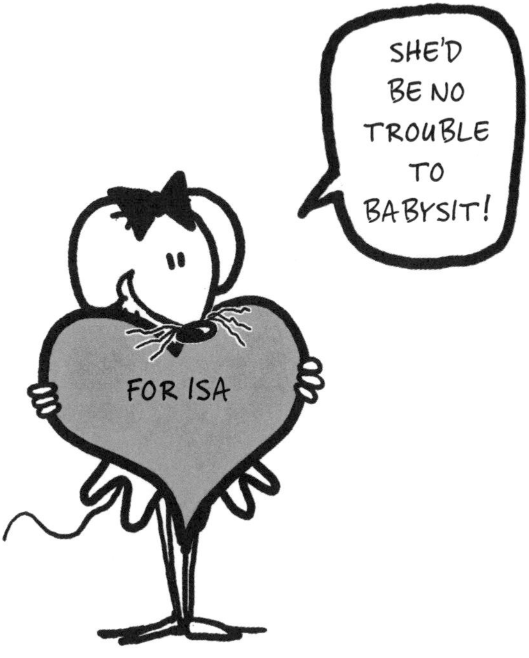
SHE'D BE NO TROUBLE TO BABYSIT!
FOR ISA

Nursery Rhyme Classics
~PRESENTS~

The Old Woman
Who Lived in a Shoe

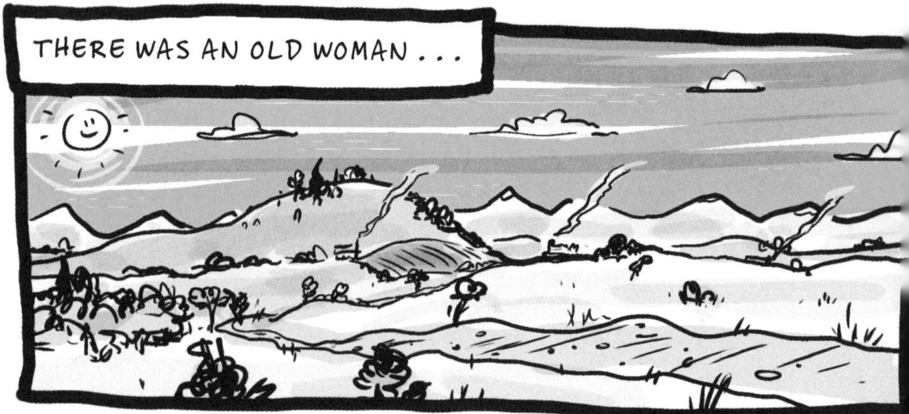
THERE WAS AN OLD WOMAN . . .

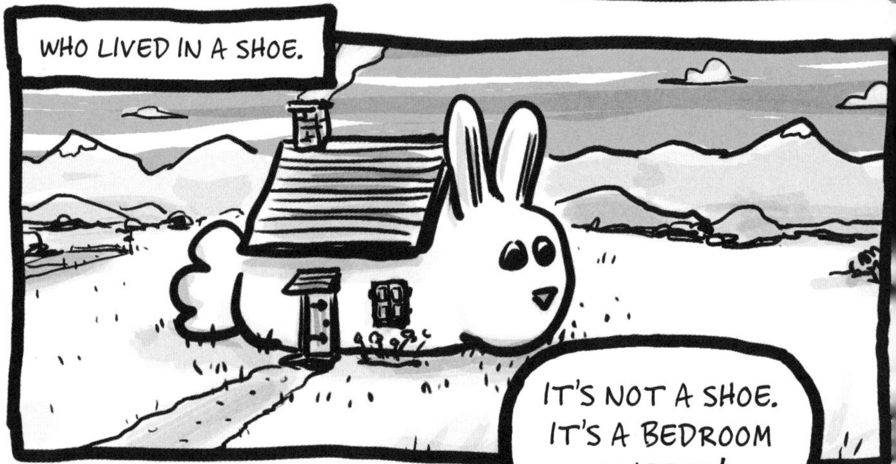
WHO LIVED IN A SHOE.

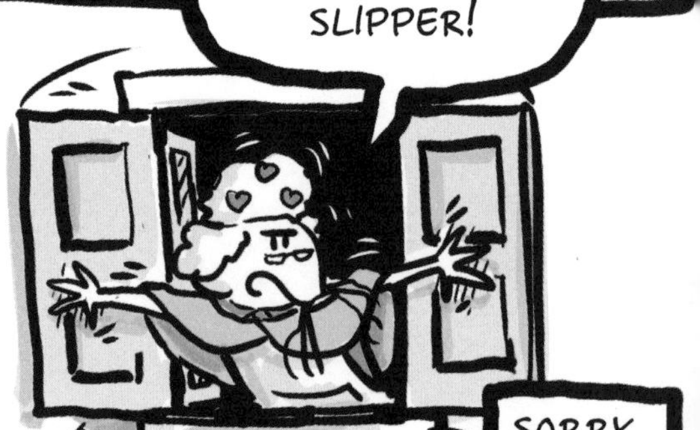
IT'S NOT A SHOE. IT'S A BEDROOM SLIPPER!
SORRY.

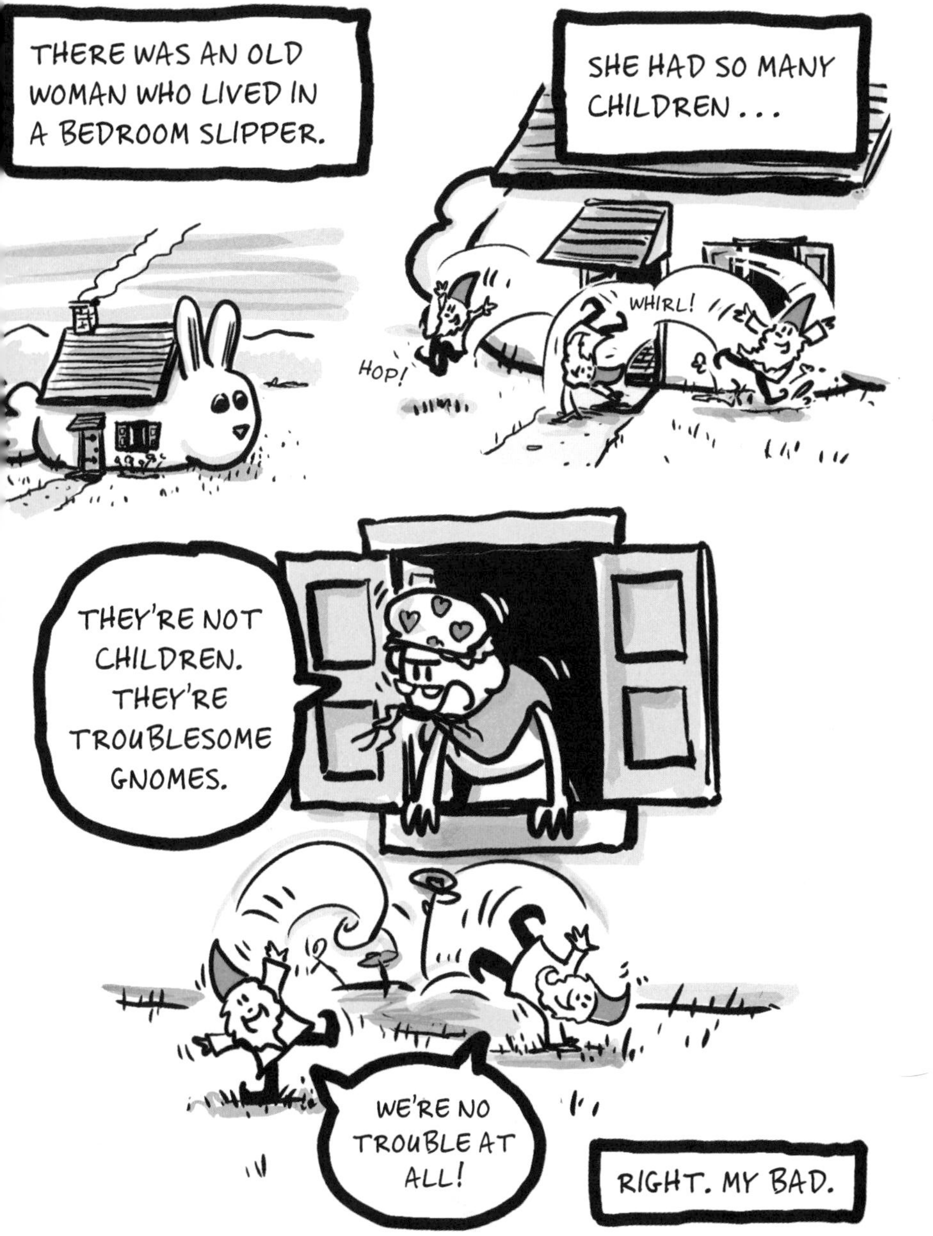
THERE WAS AN OLD WOMAN WHO LIVED IN A BEDROOM SLIPPER.
SHE HAD SO MANY CHILDREN . . .
WHIRL!
HOP!
THEY'RE NOT CHILDREN. THEY'RE TROUBLESOME GNOMES.
WE'RE NO TROUBLE AT ALL!
RIGHT. MY BAD.

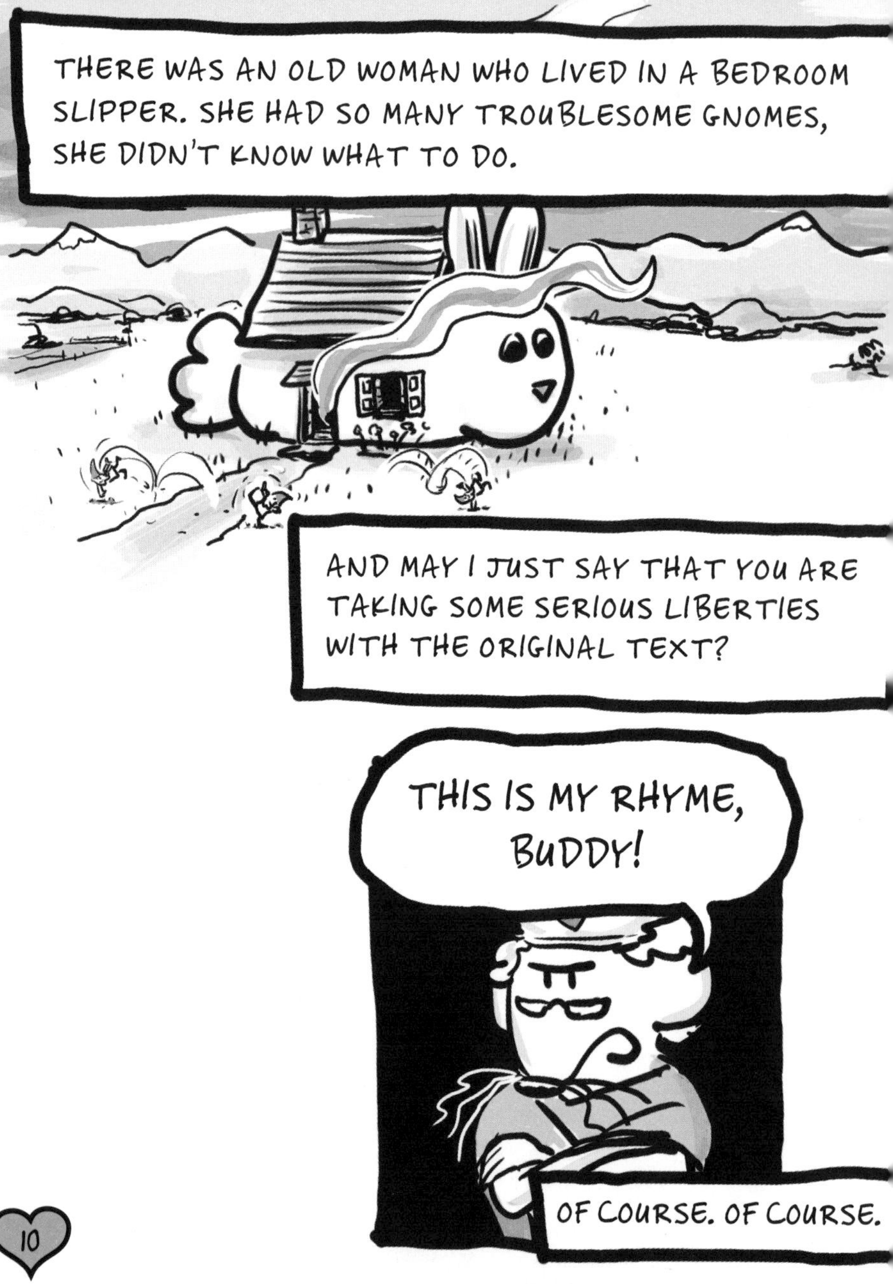
THERE WAS AN OLD WOMAN WHO LIVED IN A BEDROOM SLIPPER. SHE HAD SO MANY TROUBLESOME GNOMES, SHE DIDN'T KNOW WHAT TO DO.
AND MAY I JUST SAY THAT YOU ARE TAKING SOME SERIOUS LIBERTIES WITH THE ORIGINAL TEXT?
THIS IS MY RHYME, BUDDY!
OF COURSE. OF COURSE.

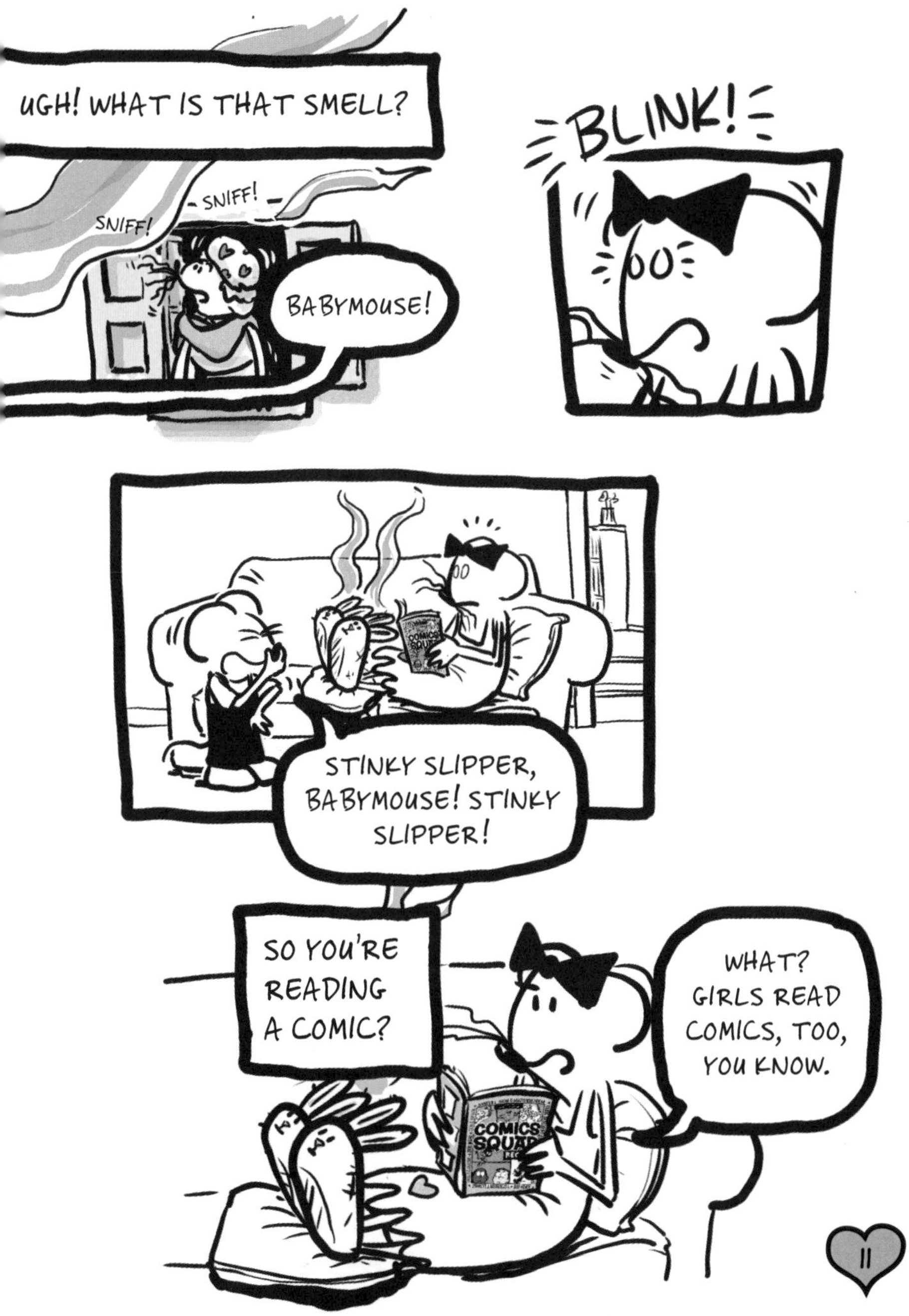

UGH! WHAT IS THAT SMELL?
SNIFF!
SNIFF!
BABYMOUSE!
BLINK!
STINKY SLIPPER, BABYMOUSE! STINKY SLIPPER!
SO YOU'RE READING A COMIC?
WHAT? GIRLS READ COMICS, TOO, YOU KNOW.
COMICS SQUAD

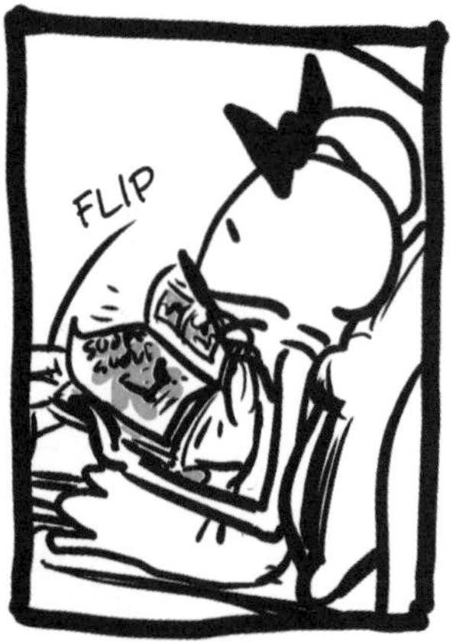
FLIP
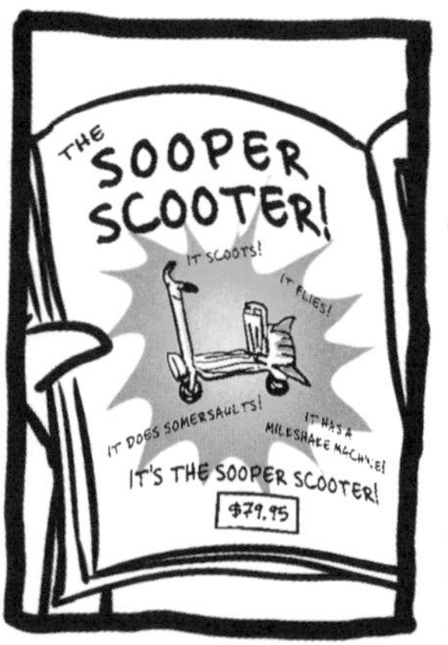
THE SOOPER SCOOTER!
IT SCOOTS!
IT FLIES!
IT DOES SOMERSAULTS!
IT HAS A MILKSHAKE MACHINE!
IT'S THE SOOPER SCOOTER!
$79.95
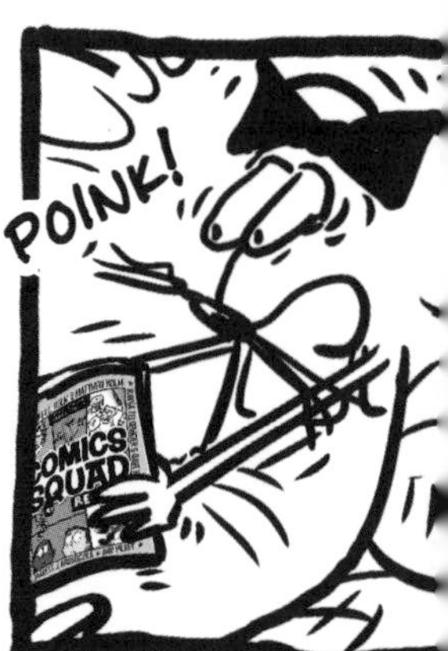
POINK!
COMICS SQUAD
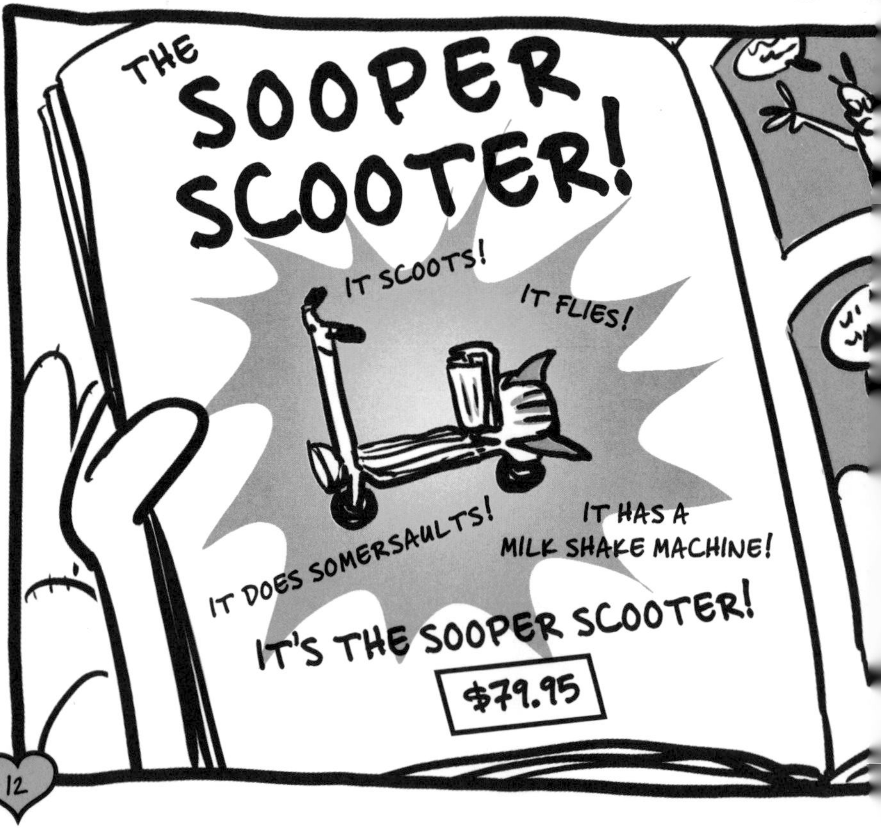
THE SOOPER SCOOTER!
IT SCOOTS!
IT FLIES!
IT DOES SOMERSAULTS!
IT HAS A MILK SHAKE MACHINE!
IT'S THE SOOPER SCOOTER!
$79.95

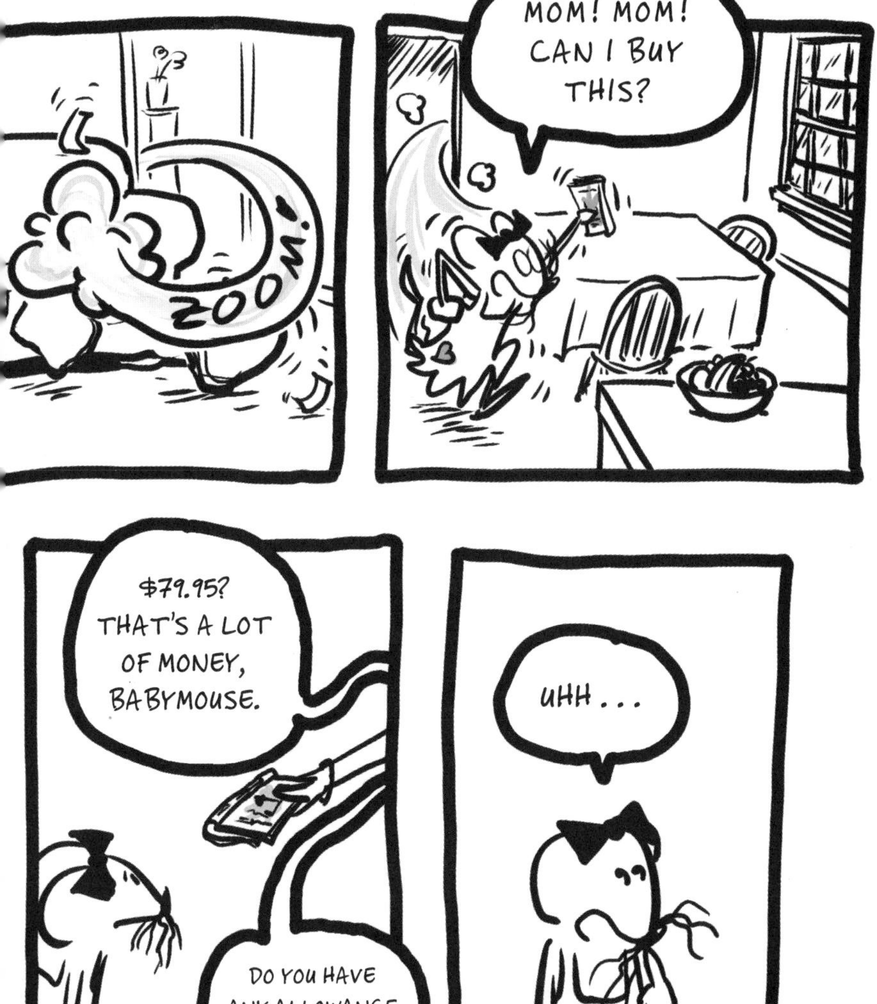
ZOOM!
MOM! MOM! CAN I BUY THIS?
$79.95? THAT'S A LOT OF MONEY, BABYMOUSE.
DO YOU HAVE ANY ALLOWANCE LEFT?
UHH . . .

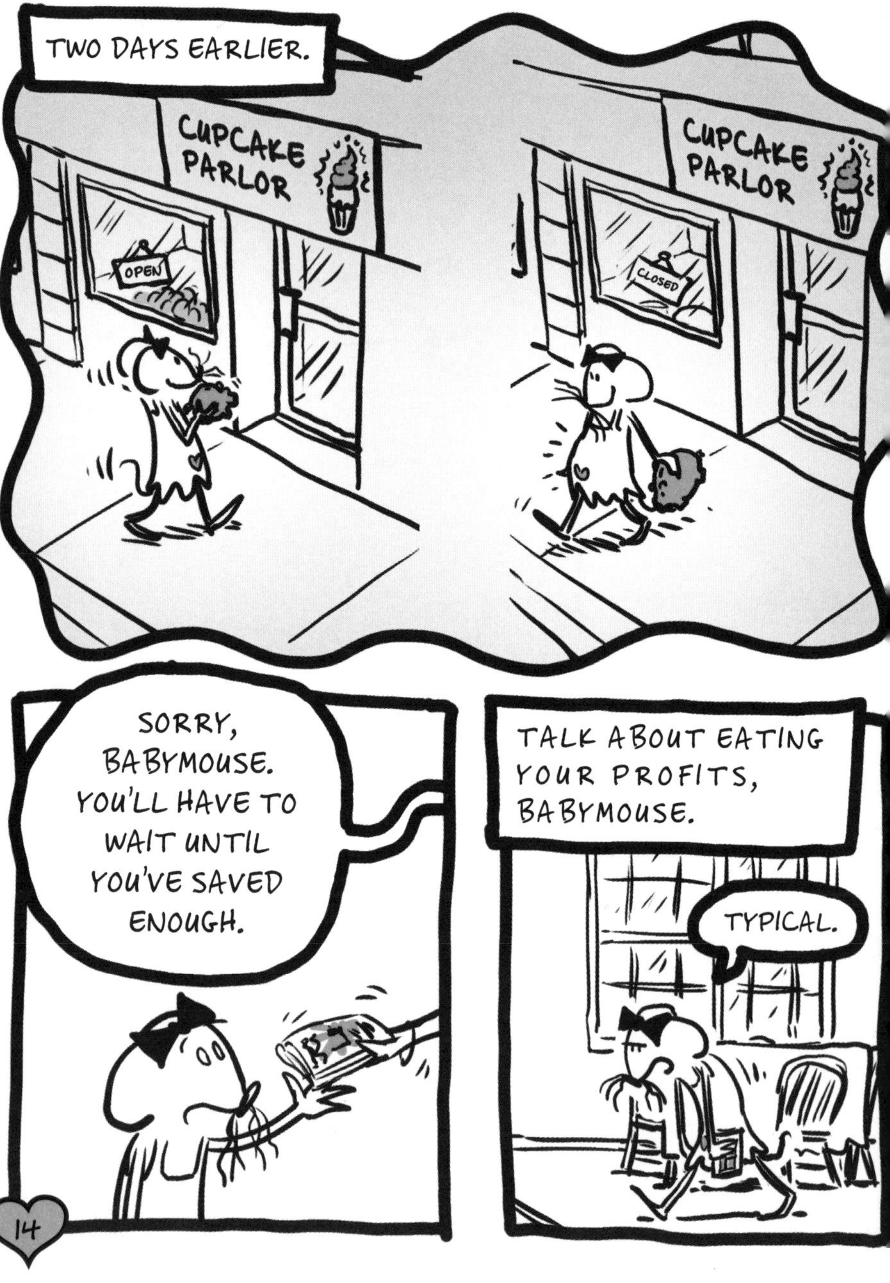
TWO DAYS EARLIER.
CUPCAKE PARLOR
OPEN
CUPCAKE PARLOR
CLOSED
SORRY, BABYMOUSE. YOU'LL HAVE TO WAIT UNTIL YOU'VE SAVED ENOUGH.
TALK ABOUT EATING YOUR PROFITS, BABYMOUSE.
TYPICAL.

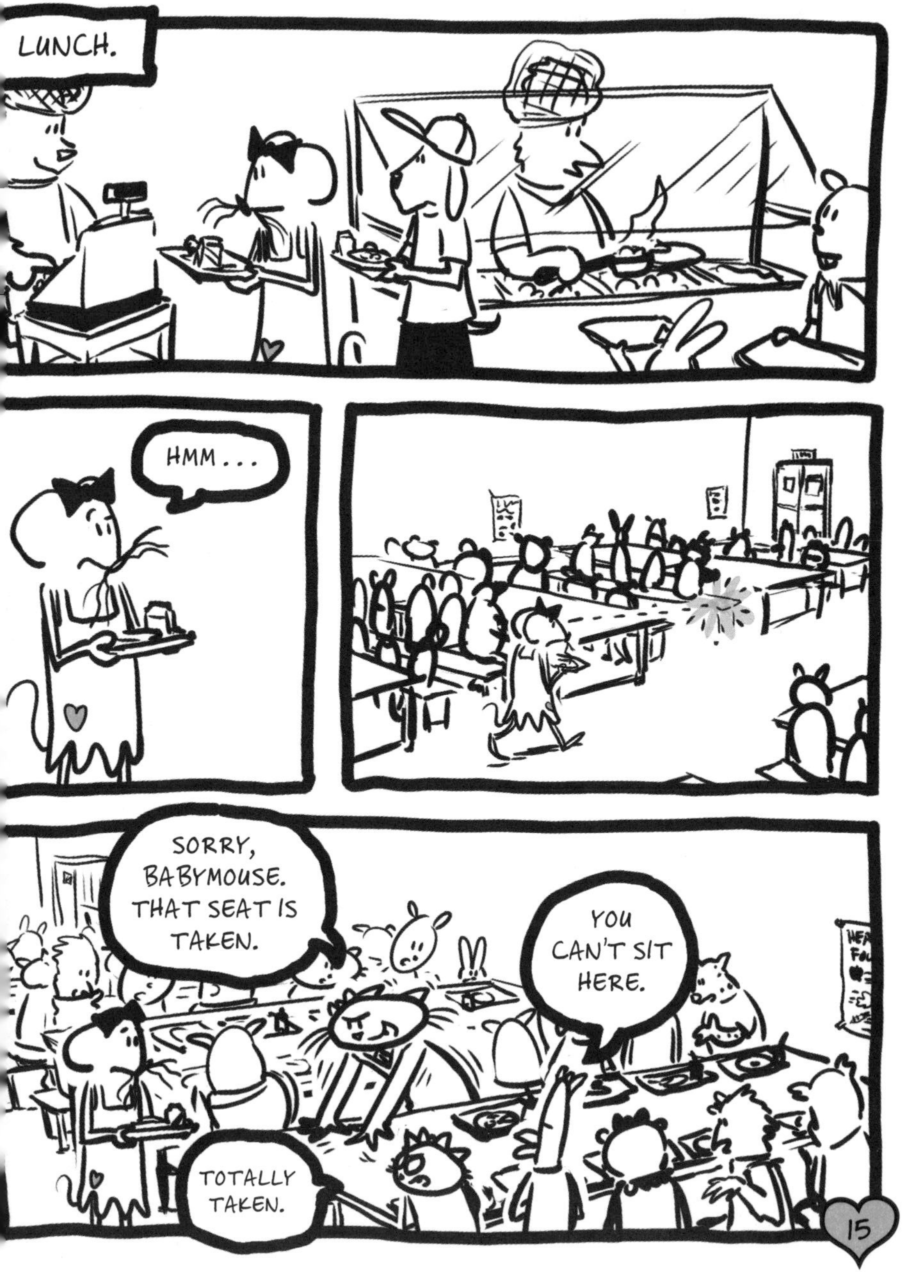
LUNCH.
HMM...
SORRY, BABYMOUSE. THAT SEAT IS TAKEN.
YOU CAN'T SIT HERE.
TOTALLY TAKEN.

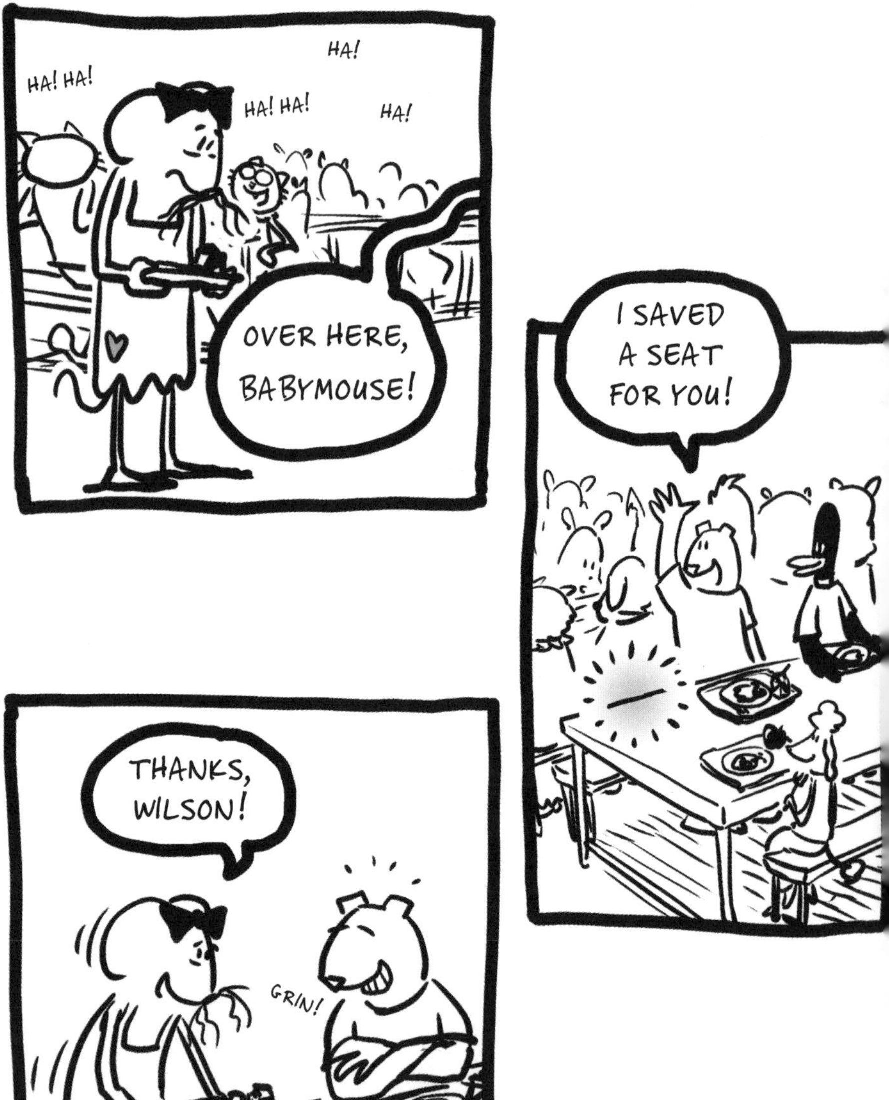
HA! HA!
HA!
HA! HA!
HA!
OVER HERE, BABYMOUSE!
I SAVED A SEAT FOR YOU!
THANKS, WILSON!
GRIN!

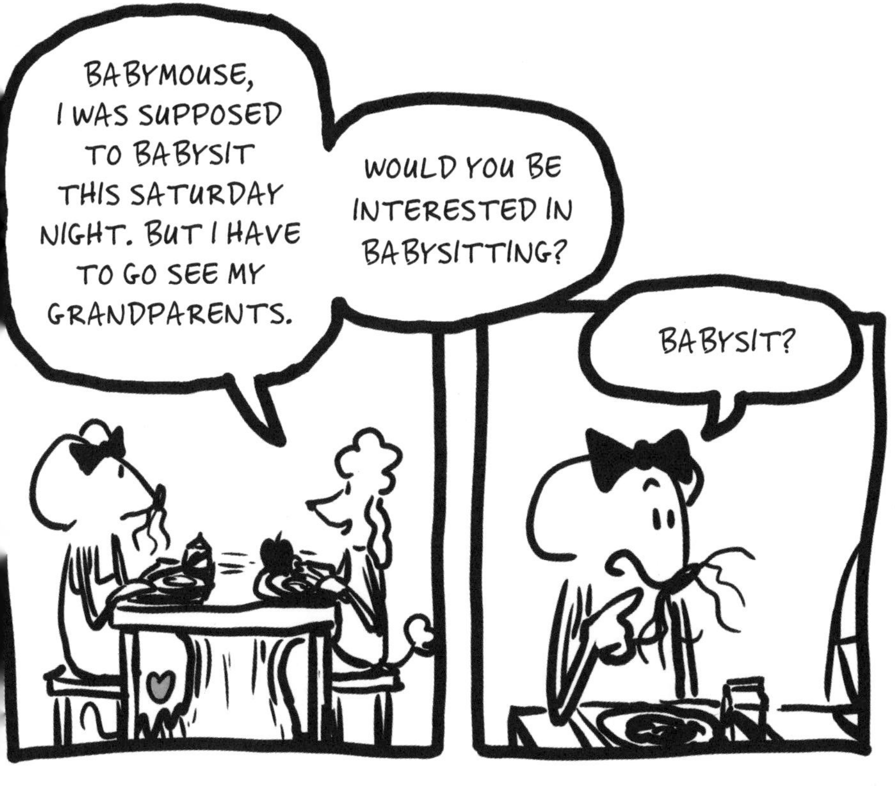
BABYMOUSE, I WAS SUPPOSED TO BABYSIT THIS SATURDAY NIGHT. BUT I HAVE TO GO SEE MY GRANDPARENTS.
WOULD YOU BE INTERESTED IN BABYSITTING?
BABYSIT?

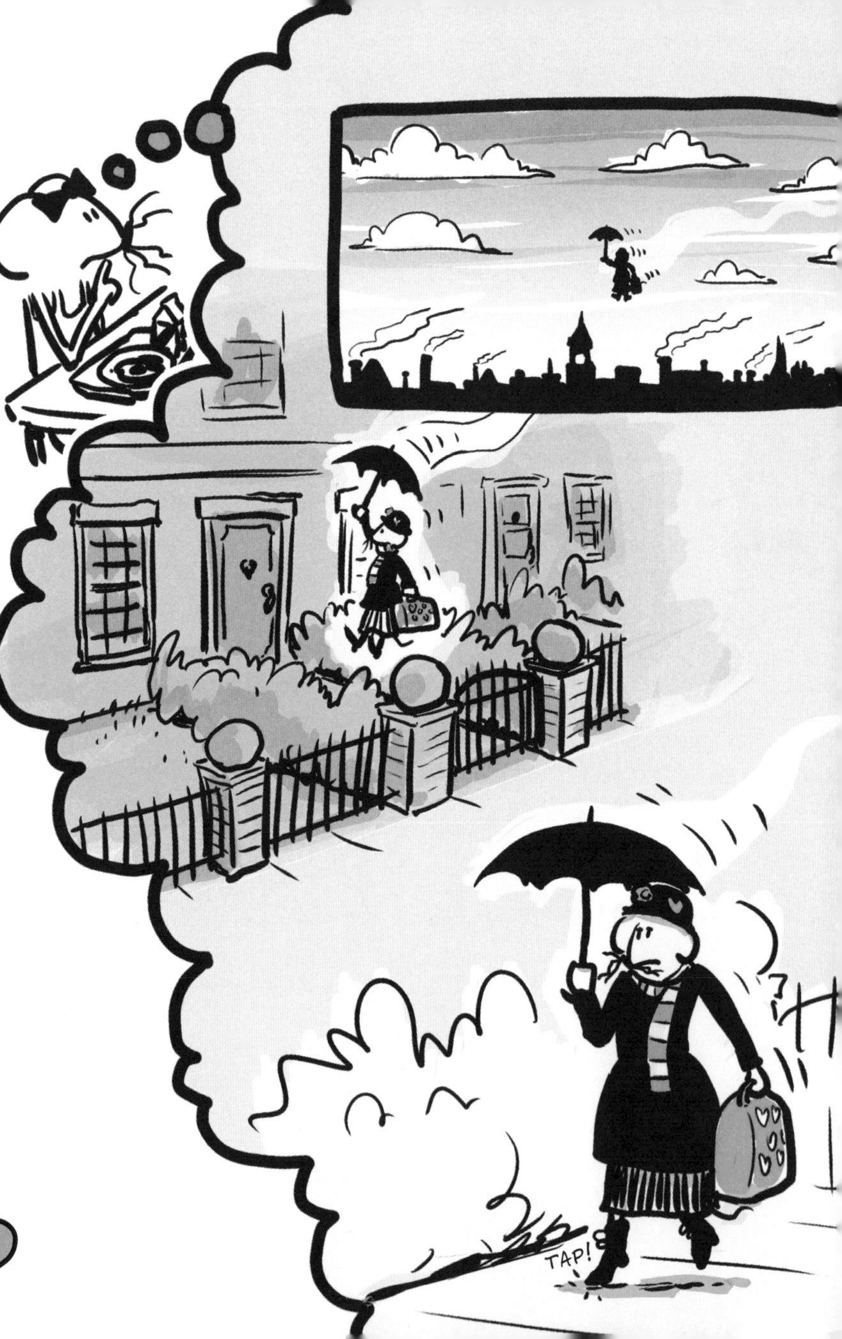
TAP!

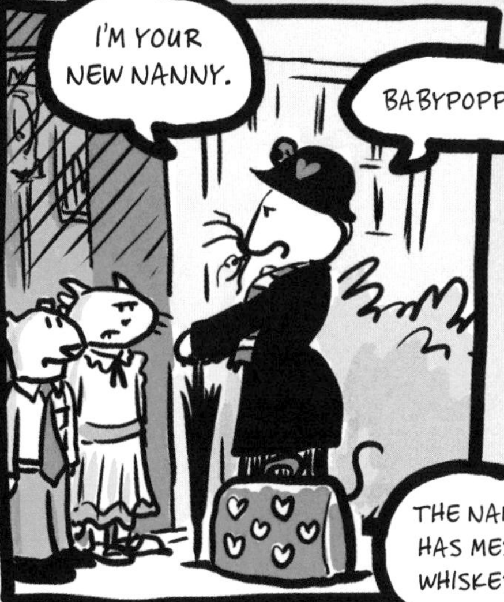
I'M YOUR NEW NANNY.
BABYPOPPINS.

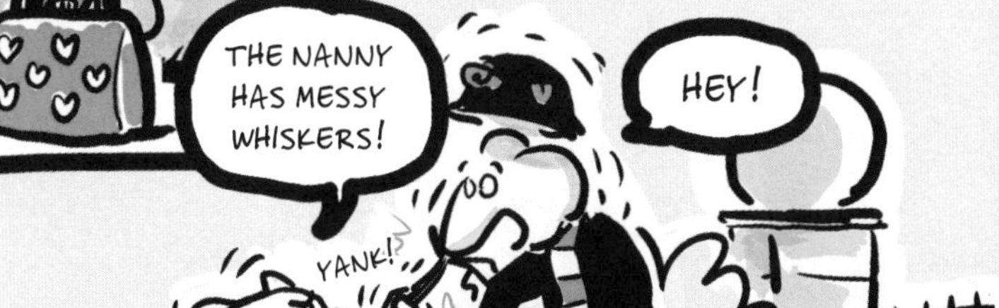
THE NANNY HAS MESSY WHISKERS!
HEY!
YANK!

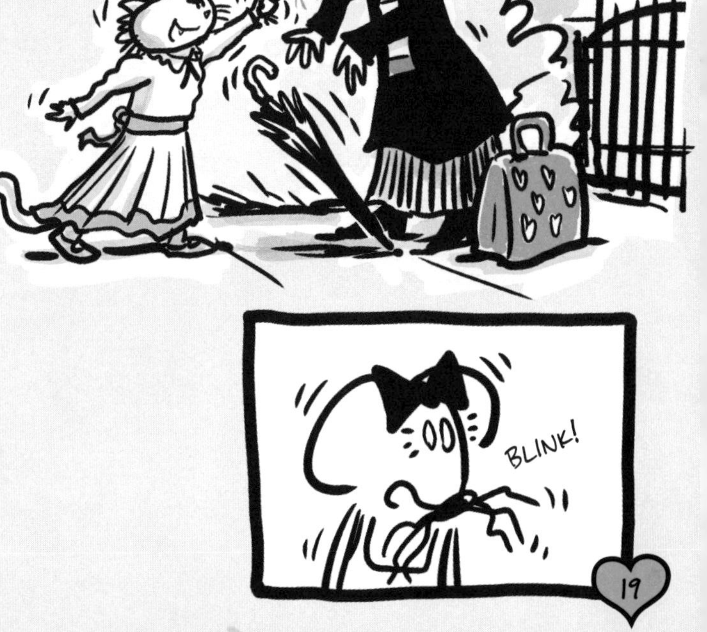
BLINK!

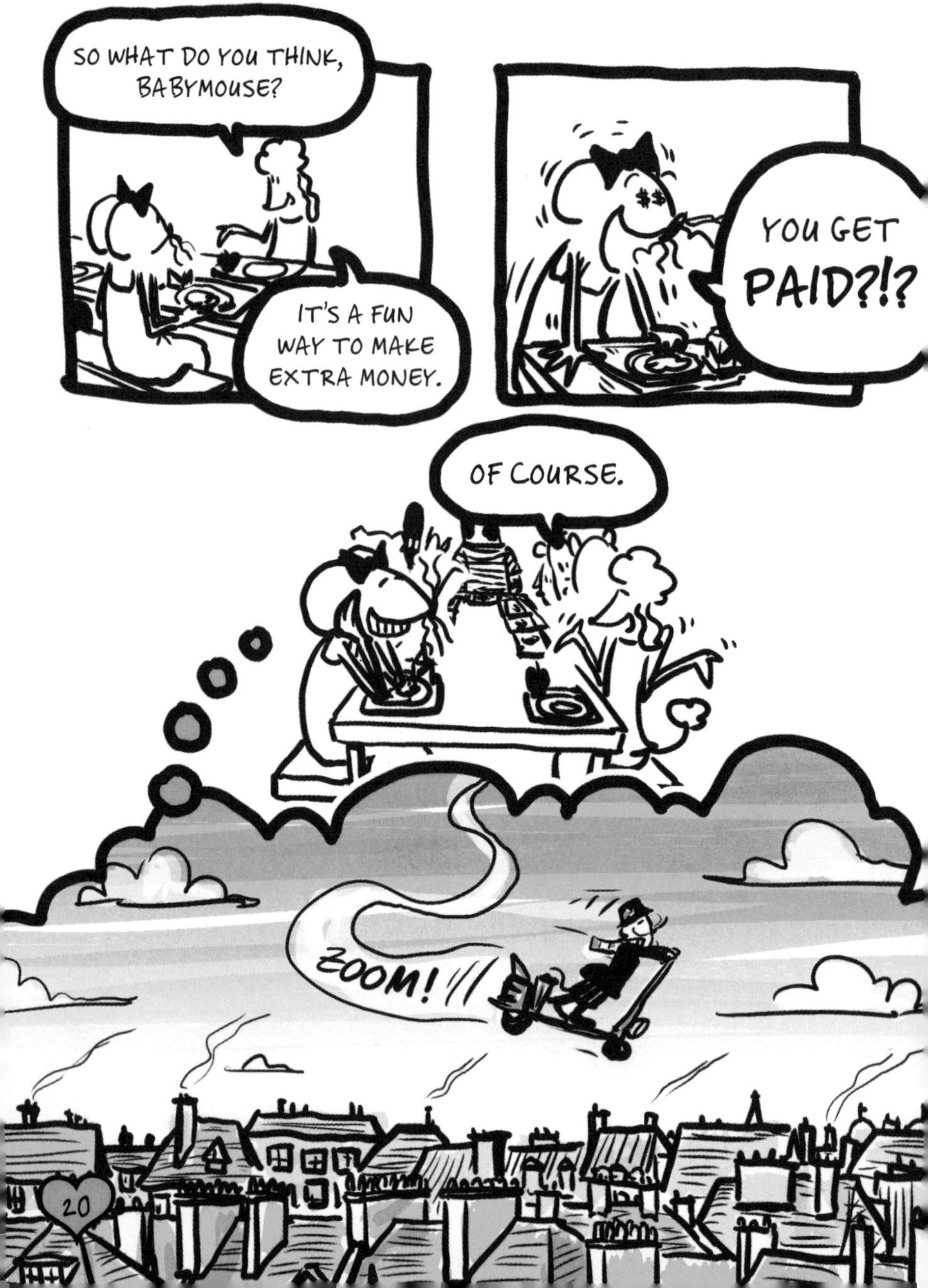
SO WHAT DO YOU THINK, BABYMOUSE?
IT'S A FUN WAY TO MAKE EXTRA MONEY.
YOU GET PAID?!?
OF COURSE.
ZOOM!

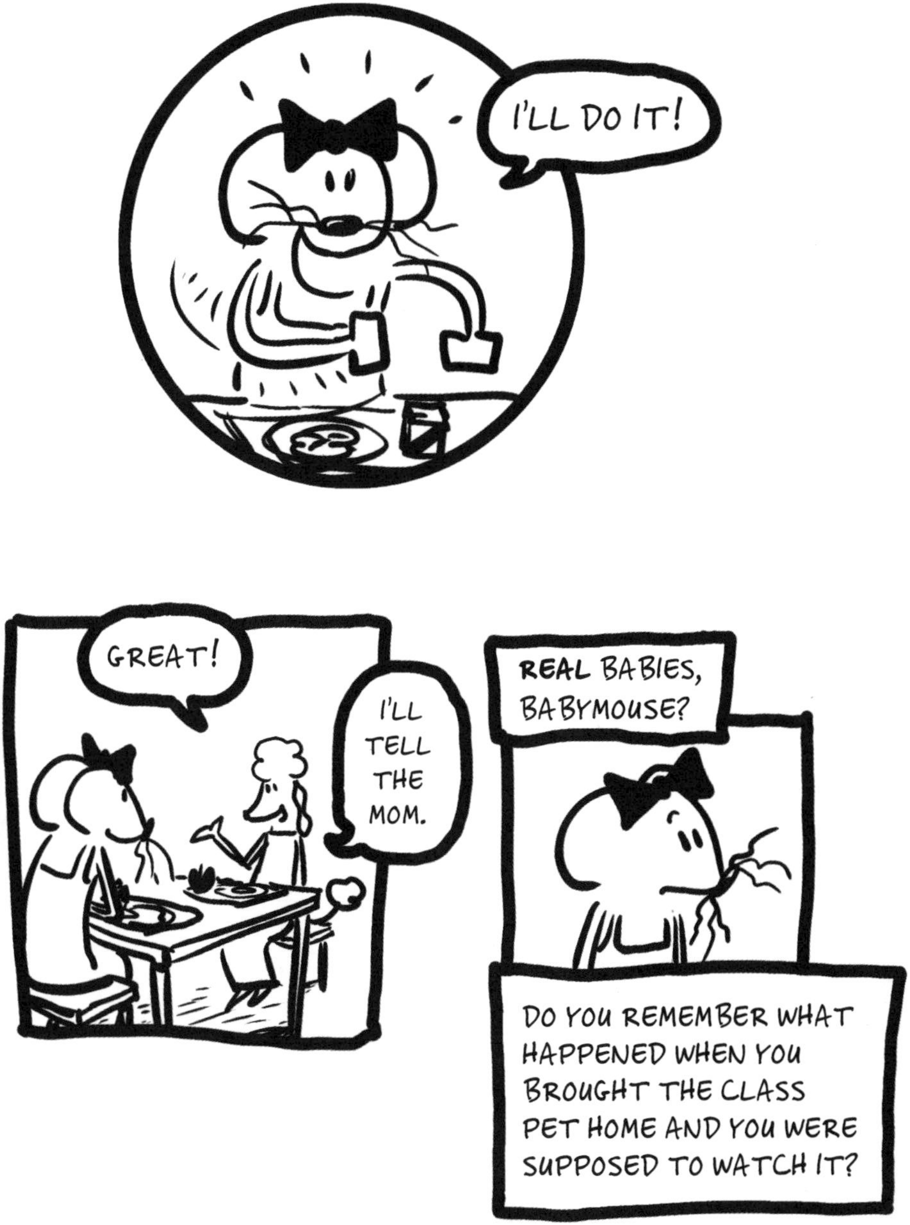
I'LL DO IT!
GREAT!
I'LL TELL THE MOM.
REAL BABIES, BABYMOUSE?
DO YOU REMEMBER WHAT HAPPENED WHEN YOU BROUGHT THE CLASS PET HOME AND YOU WERE SUPPOSED TO WATCH IT?

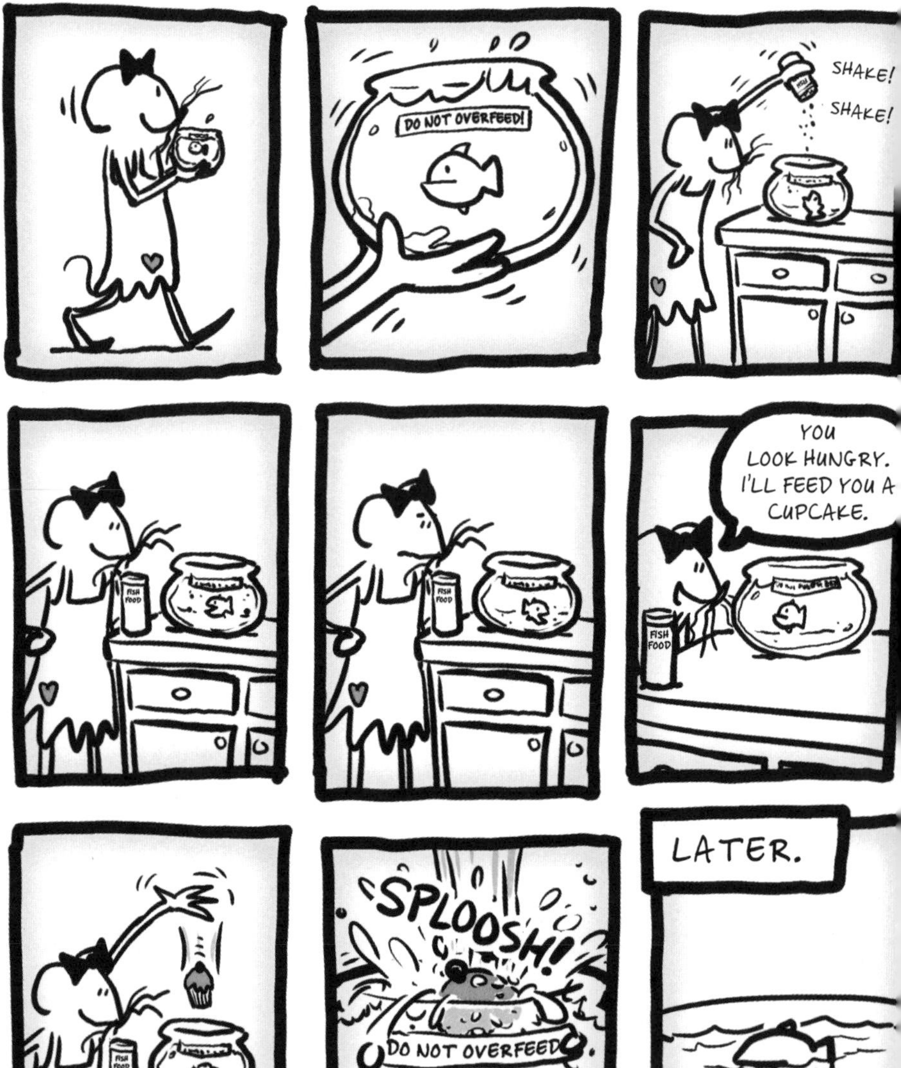
DO NOT OVERFEED!
SHAKE!
SHAKE!
FISH FOOD
FISH FOOD
YOU LOOK HUNGRY. I'LL FEED YOU A CUPCAKE.
FISH FOOD
FISH FOOD
SPLOOSH!
DO NOT OVERFEED
LATER.

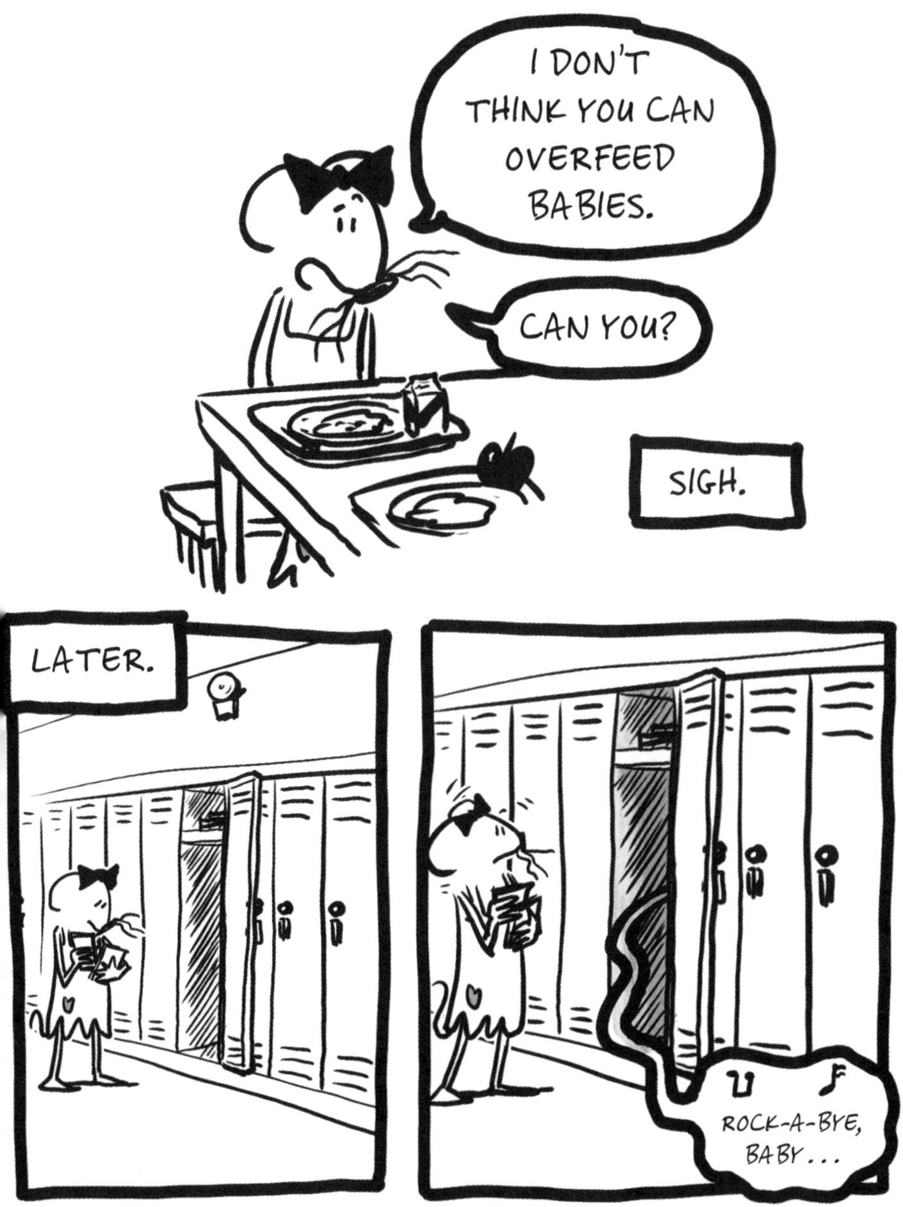
I DON'T THINK YOU CAN OVERFEED BABIES.
CAN YOU?
SIGH.
LATER.
ROCK-A-BYE, BABY . . .

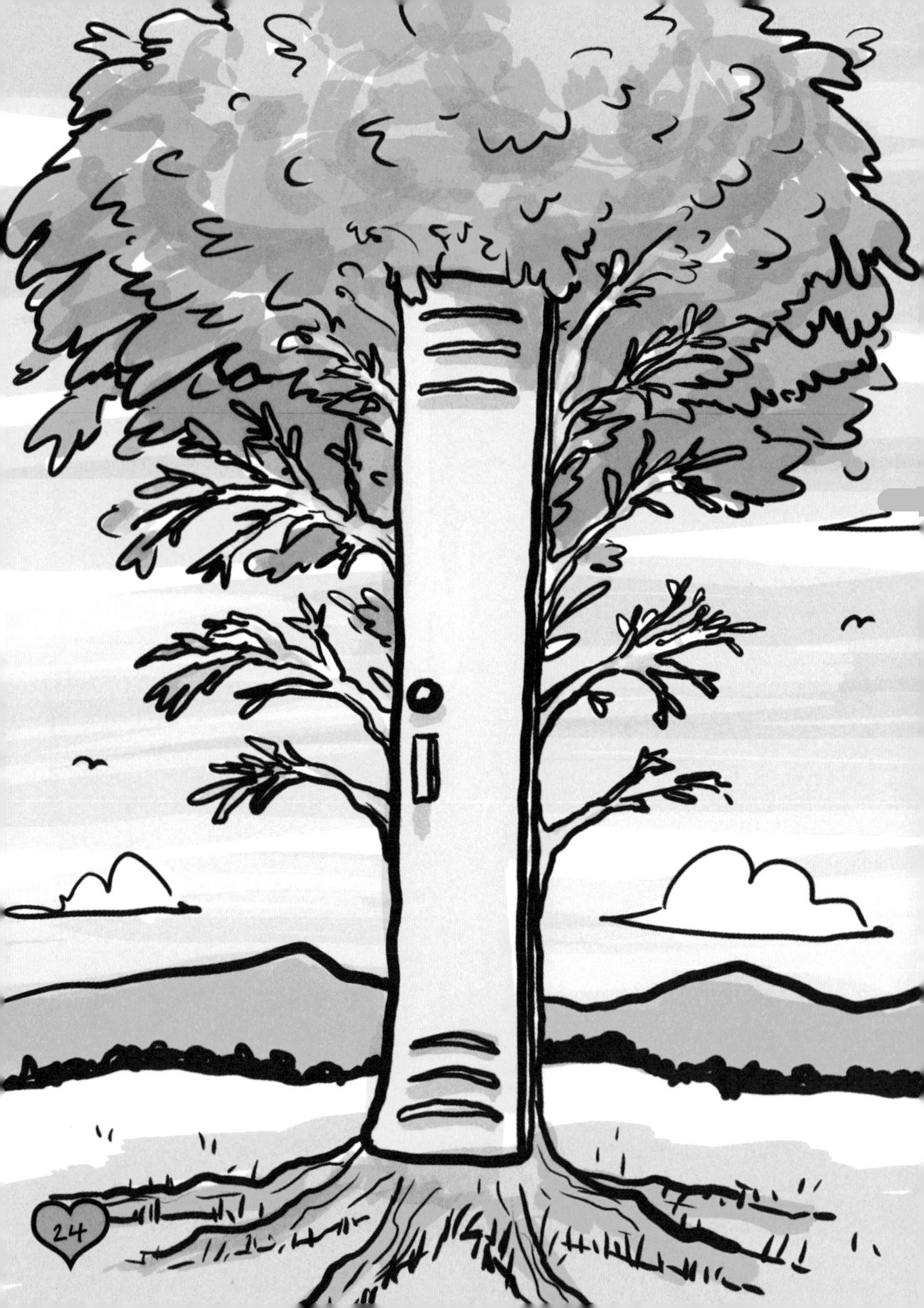

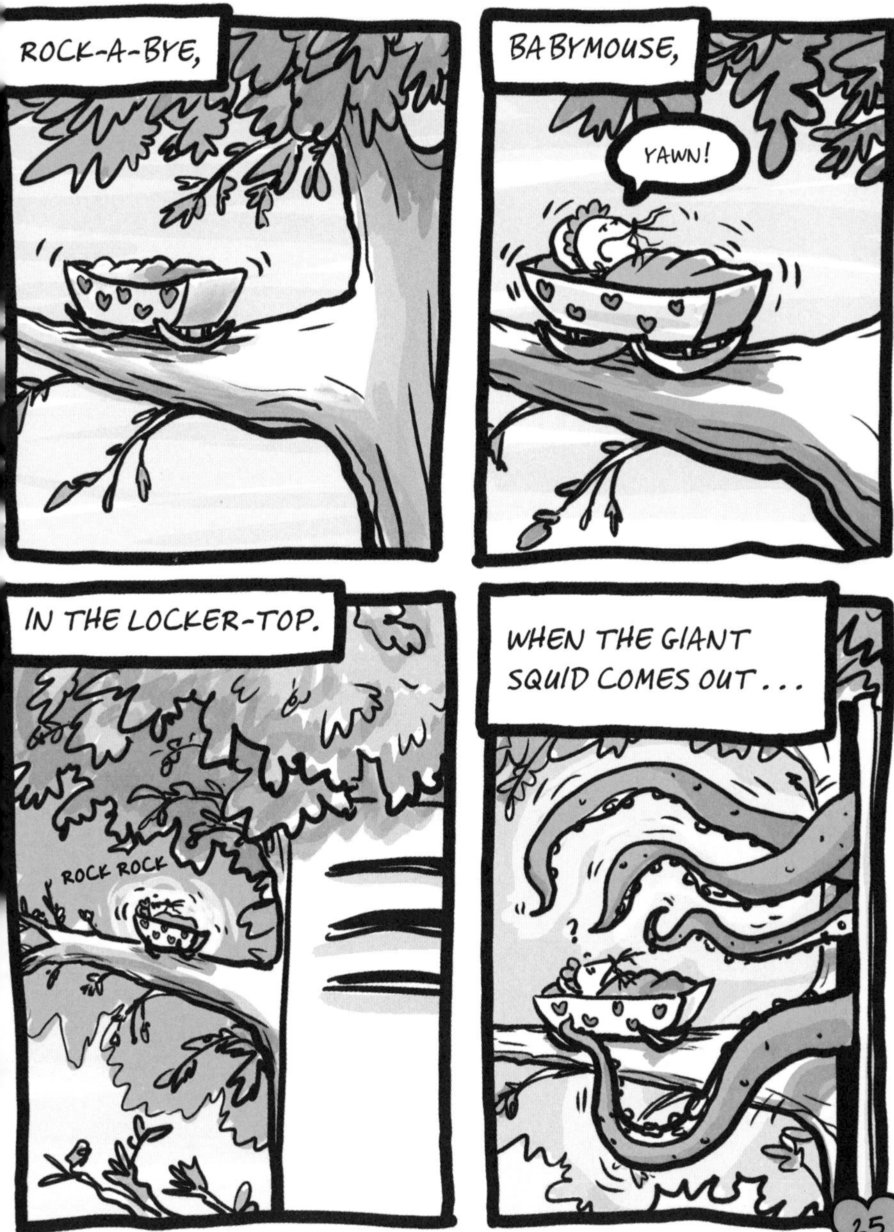
ROCK-A-BYE,
BABYMOUSE,
YAWN!
IN THE LOCKER-TOP.
ROCK ROCK
WHEN THE GIANT SQUID COMES OUT . . .
?

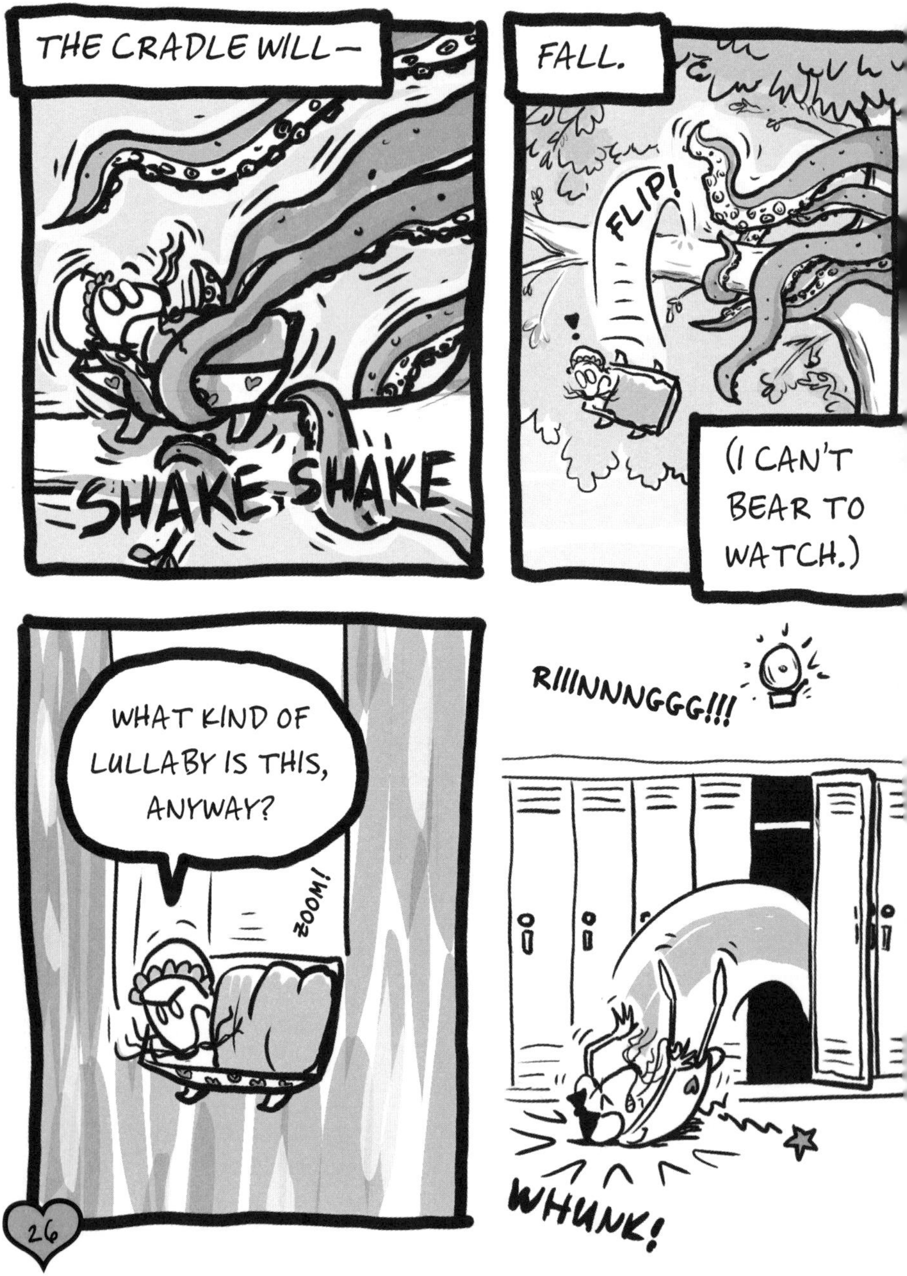
THE CRADLE WILL—
SHAKE, SHAKE
FALL.
FLIP!
(I CAN'T BEAR TO WATCH.)
WHAT KIND OF LULLABY IS THIS, ANYWAY?
ZOOM!
RIIINNNGGG!!!
WHUNK!

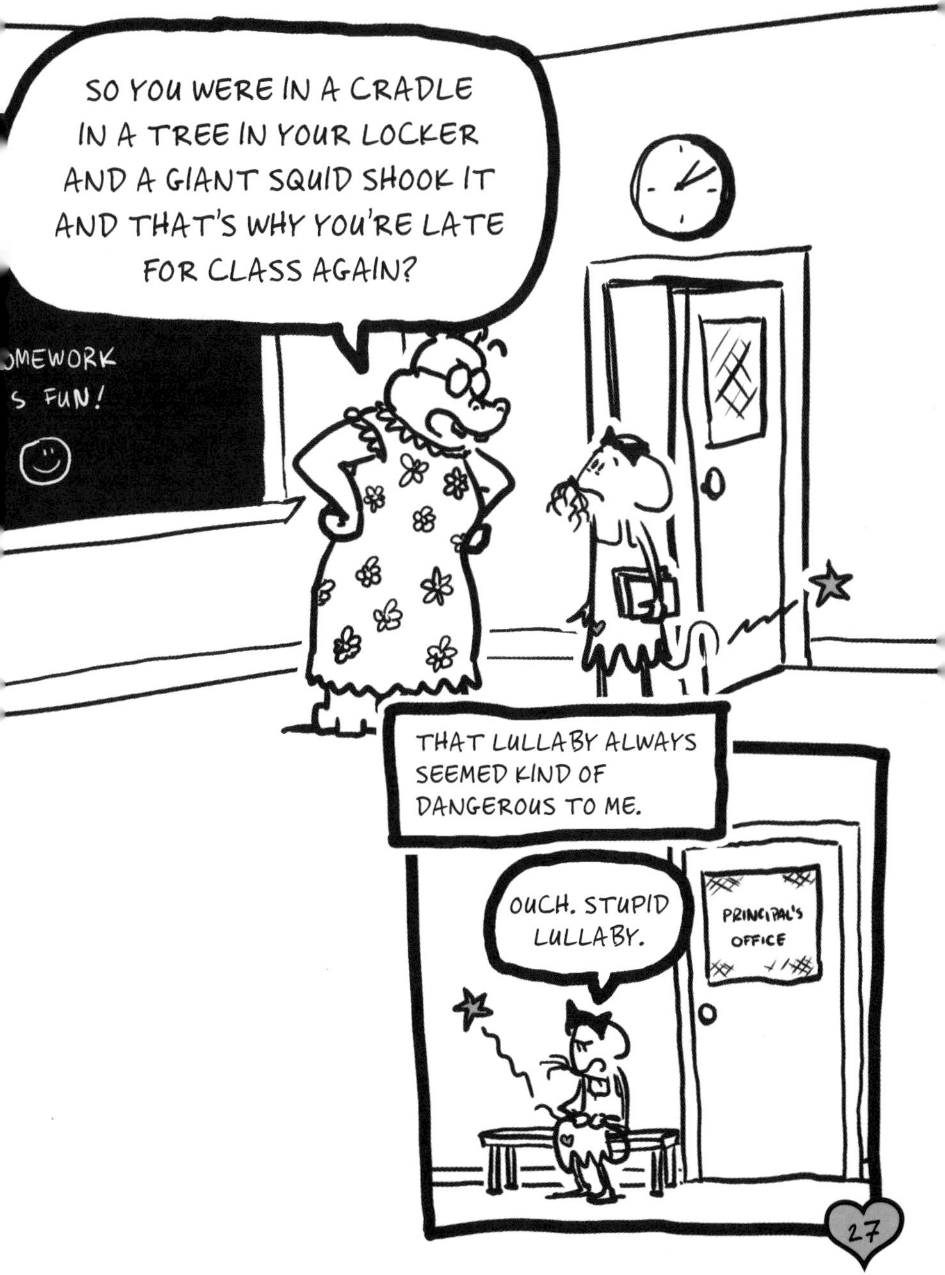
SO YOU WERE IN A CRADLE IN A TREE IN YOUR LOCKER AND A GIANT SQUID SHOOK IT AND THAT'S WHY YOU'RE LATE FOR CLASS AGAIN?
OMEWORK S FUN!
THAT LULLABY ALWAYS SEEMED KIND OF DANGEROUS TO ME.
OUCH. STUPID LULLABY.
PRINCIPAL'S OFFICE

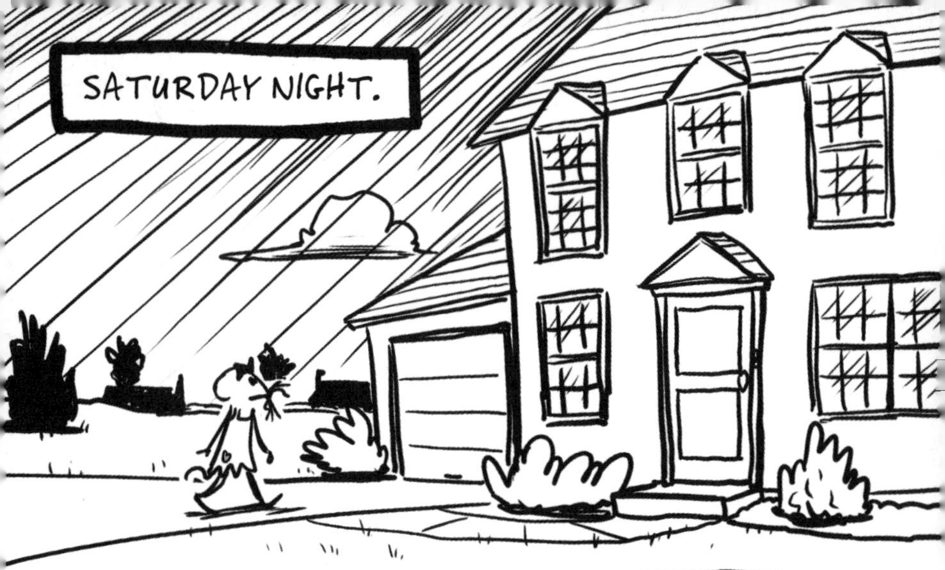
SATURDAY NIGHT.

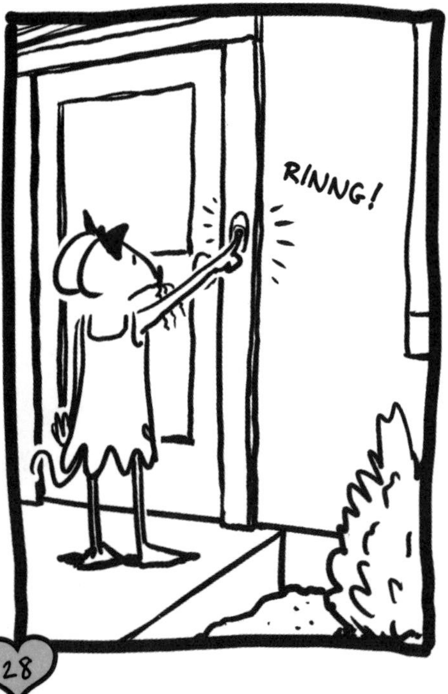
RINNG!

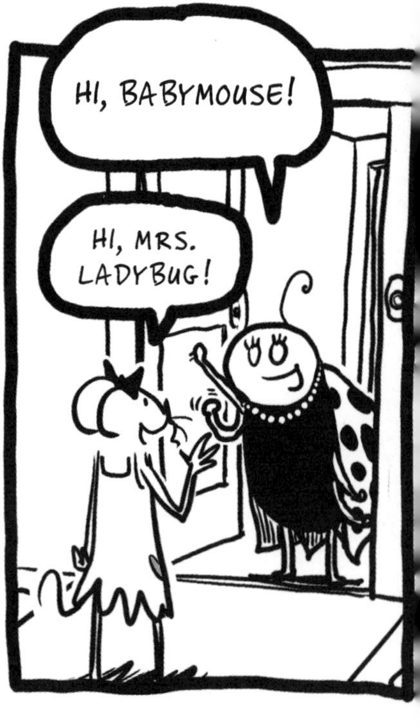
HI, BABYMOUSE!
HI, MRS. LADYBUG!

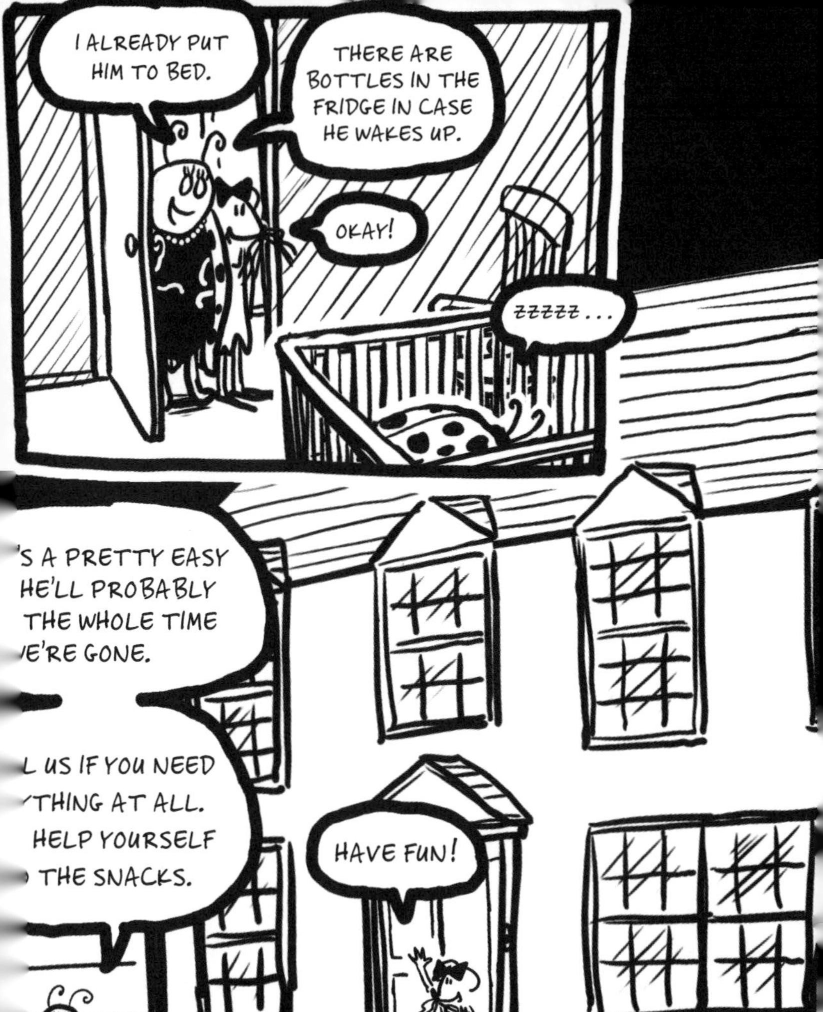
I ALREADY PUT HIM TO BED.
THERE ARE BOTTLES IN THE FRIDGE IN CASE HE WAKES UP.
OKAY!
ZZZZZ . . .
S A PRETTY EASY HE'LL PROBABLY THE WHOLE TIME RE GONE.
L US IF YOU NEED THING AT ALL. HELP YOURSELF THE SNACKS.
HAVE FUN!

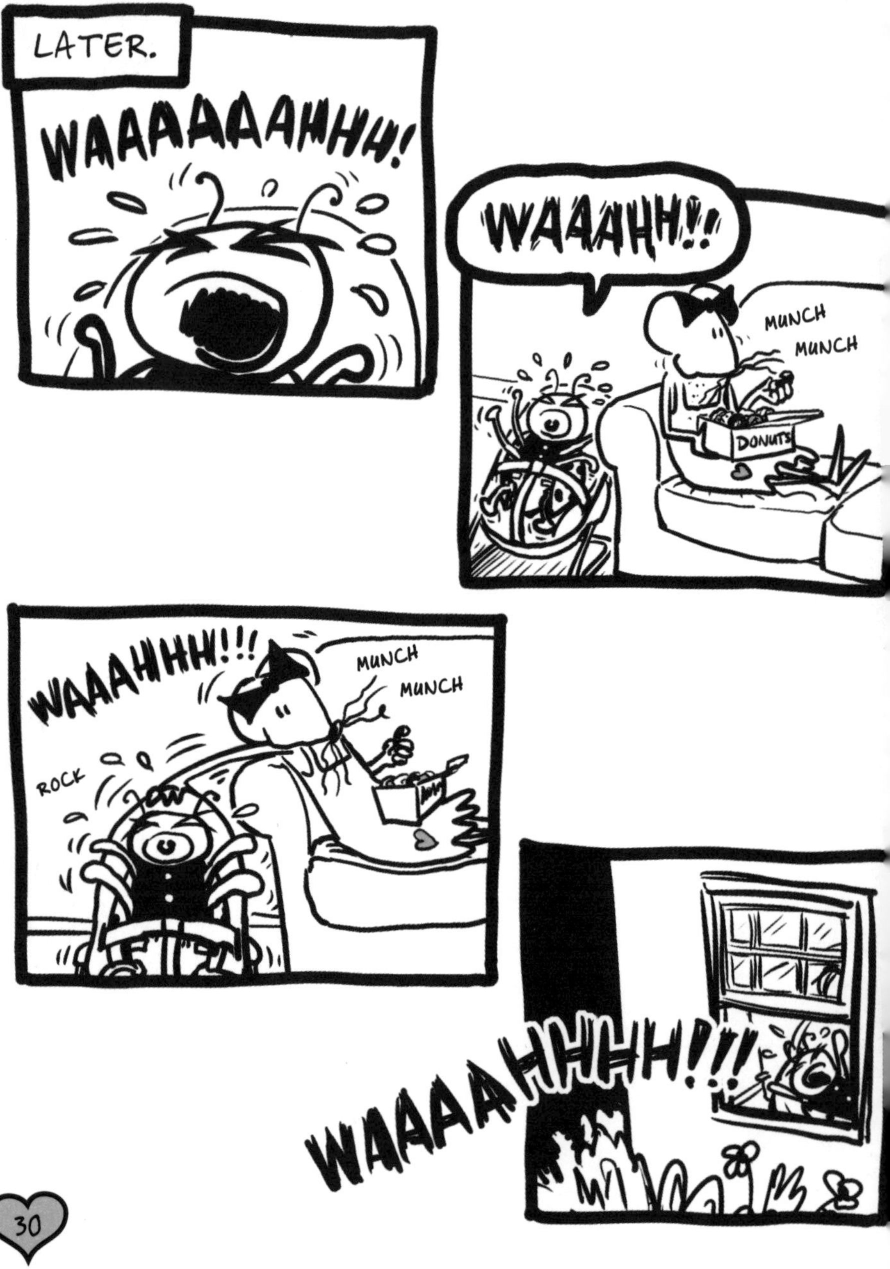

LATER.
WAAAAAAAHHH!
WAAAHH!!
MUNCH
MUNCH
DONUTS
WAAAHHH!!!
MUNCH
MUNCH
ROCK
WAAAAAHHHHH!!!

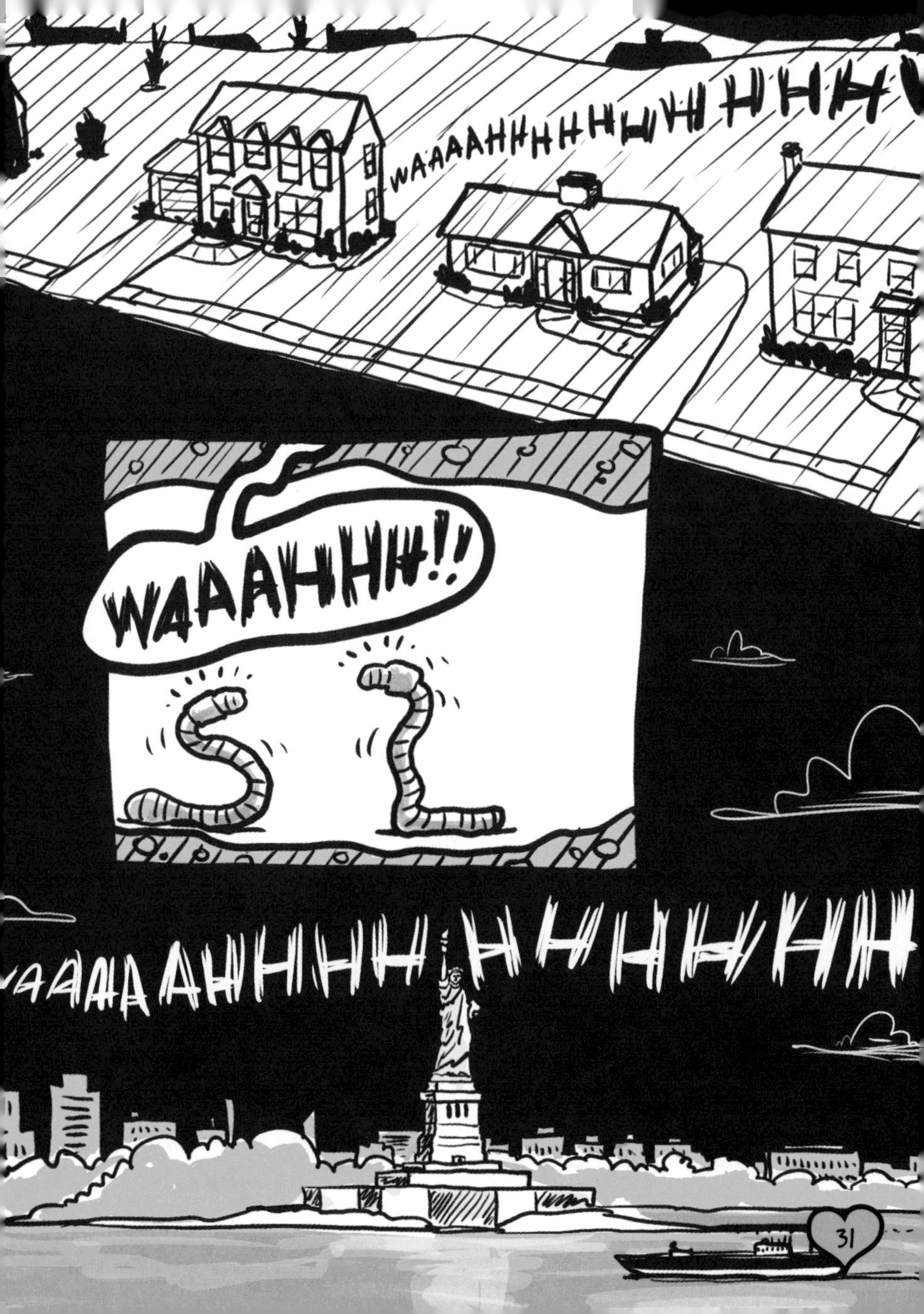
WAAAAHHHHHHHHHHHHHHHH
WAAAHHHH!!
AAAAAAHHHHHH HHHHHHHH

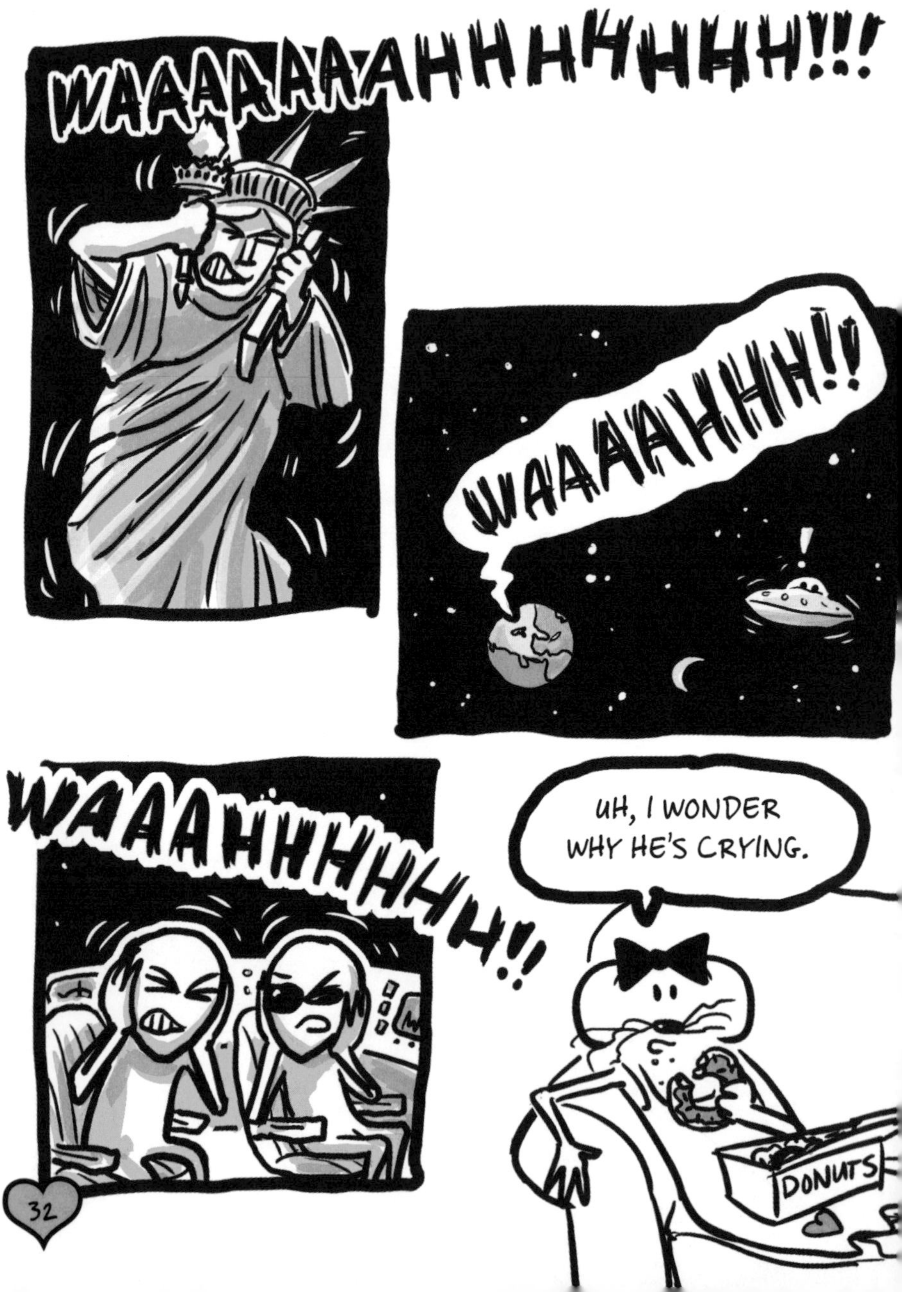
WAAAAAAAHHHHHHH!!!
WAAAAHHHH!!
WAAAHHHHHHH!!
UH, I WONDER WHY HE'S CRYING.
DONUTS

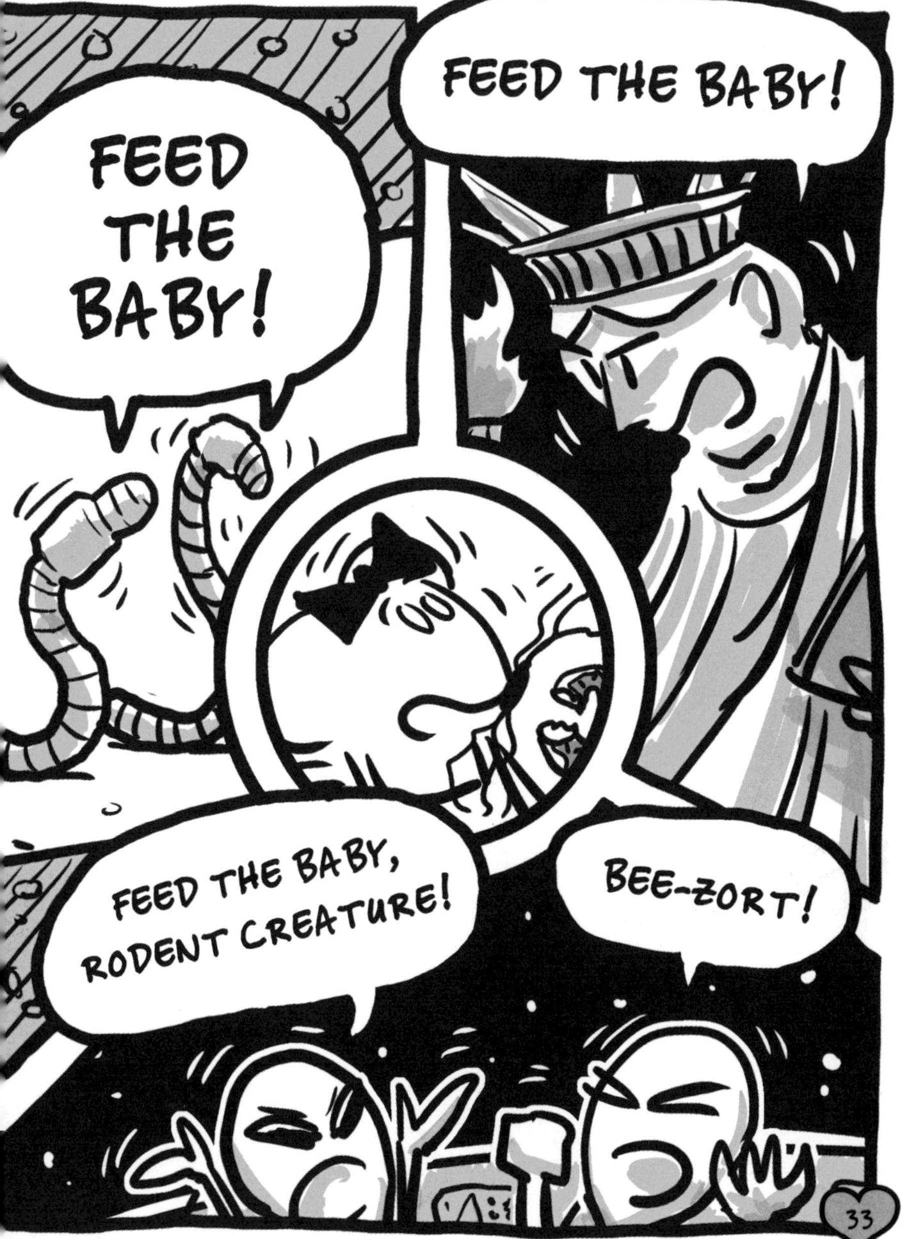
FEED THE BABY!
FEED THE BABY!
FEED THE BABY, RODENT CREATURE!
BEE-ZORT!

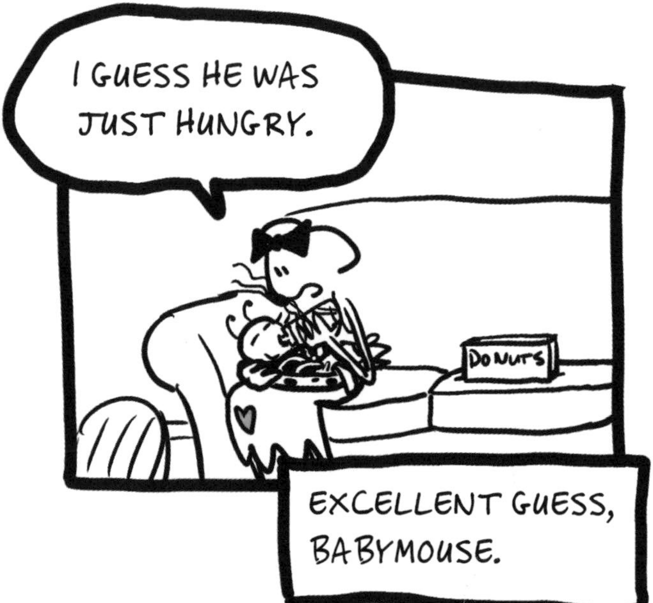
I GUESS HE WAS JUST HUNGRY.
DONUTS
EXCELLENT GUESS, BABYMOUSE.

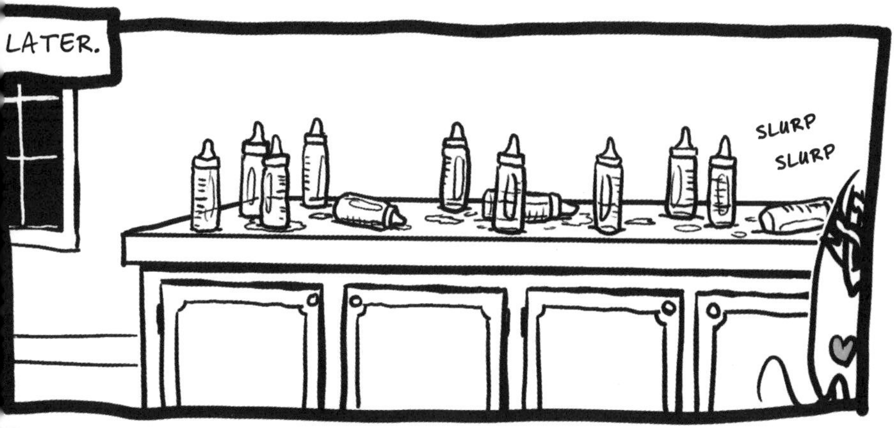
LATER.
SLURP
SLURP

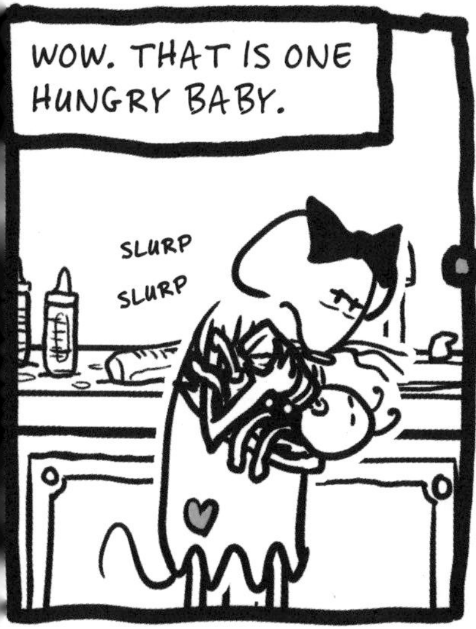
WOW. THAT IS ONE HUNGRY BABY.
SLURP
SLURP

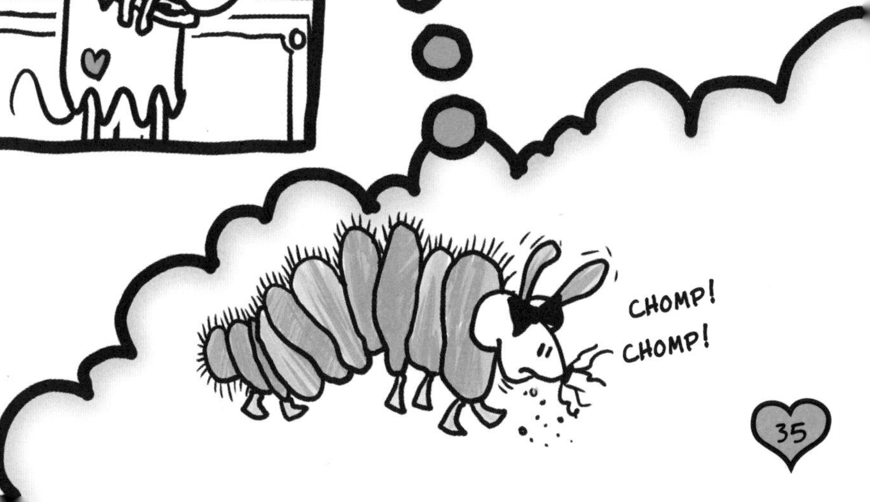
CHOMP!
CHOMP!

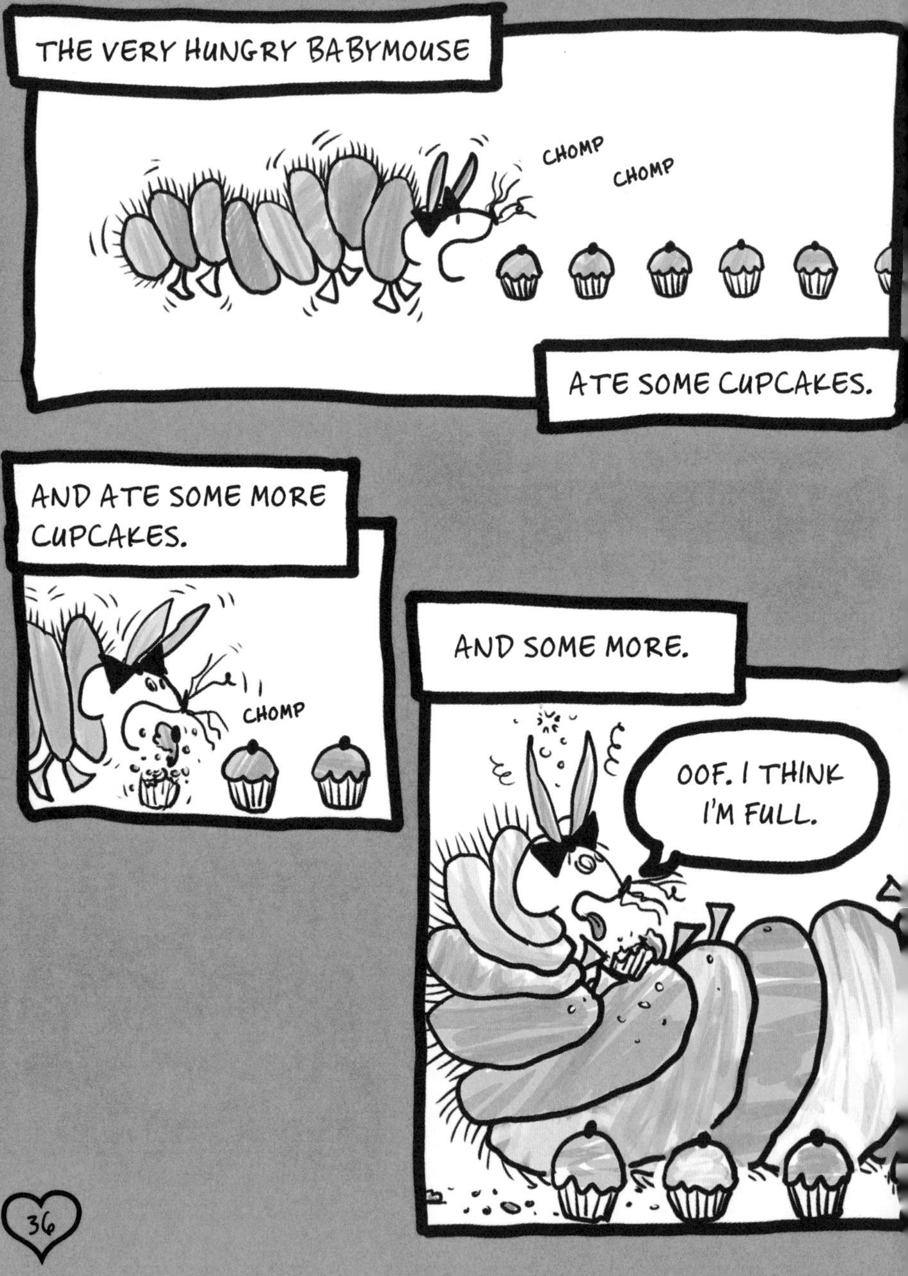

THE VERY HUNGRY BABYMOUSE
CHOMP
CHOMP
ATE SOME CUPCAKES.
AND ATE SOME MORE CUPCAKES.
CHOMP
AND SOME MORE.
OOF. I THINK I'M FULL.

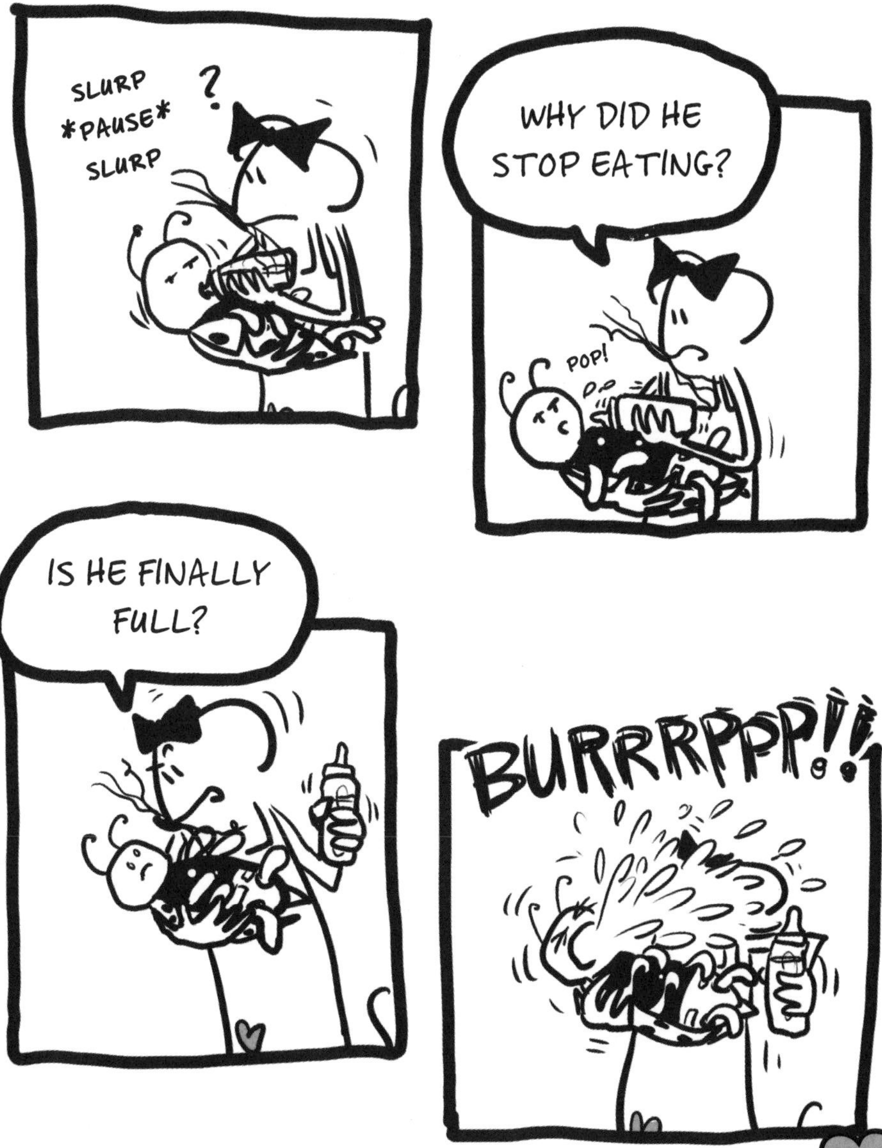
SLURP
PAUSE
SLURP
?
WHY DID HE STOP EATING?
POP!
IS HE FINALLY FULL?
BURRRPPP!!

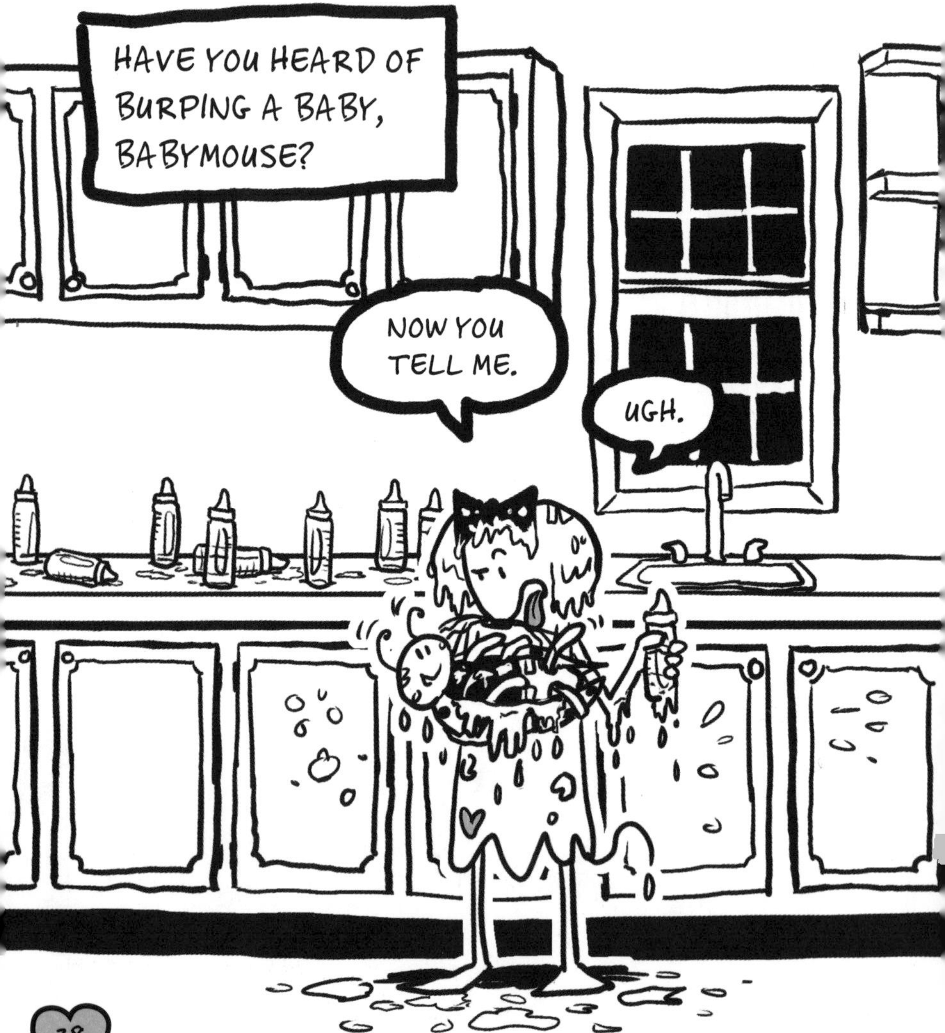
HAVE YOU HEARD OF BURPING A BABY, BABYMOUSE?
NOW YOU TELL ME.
UGH.

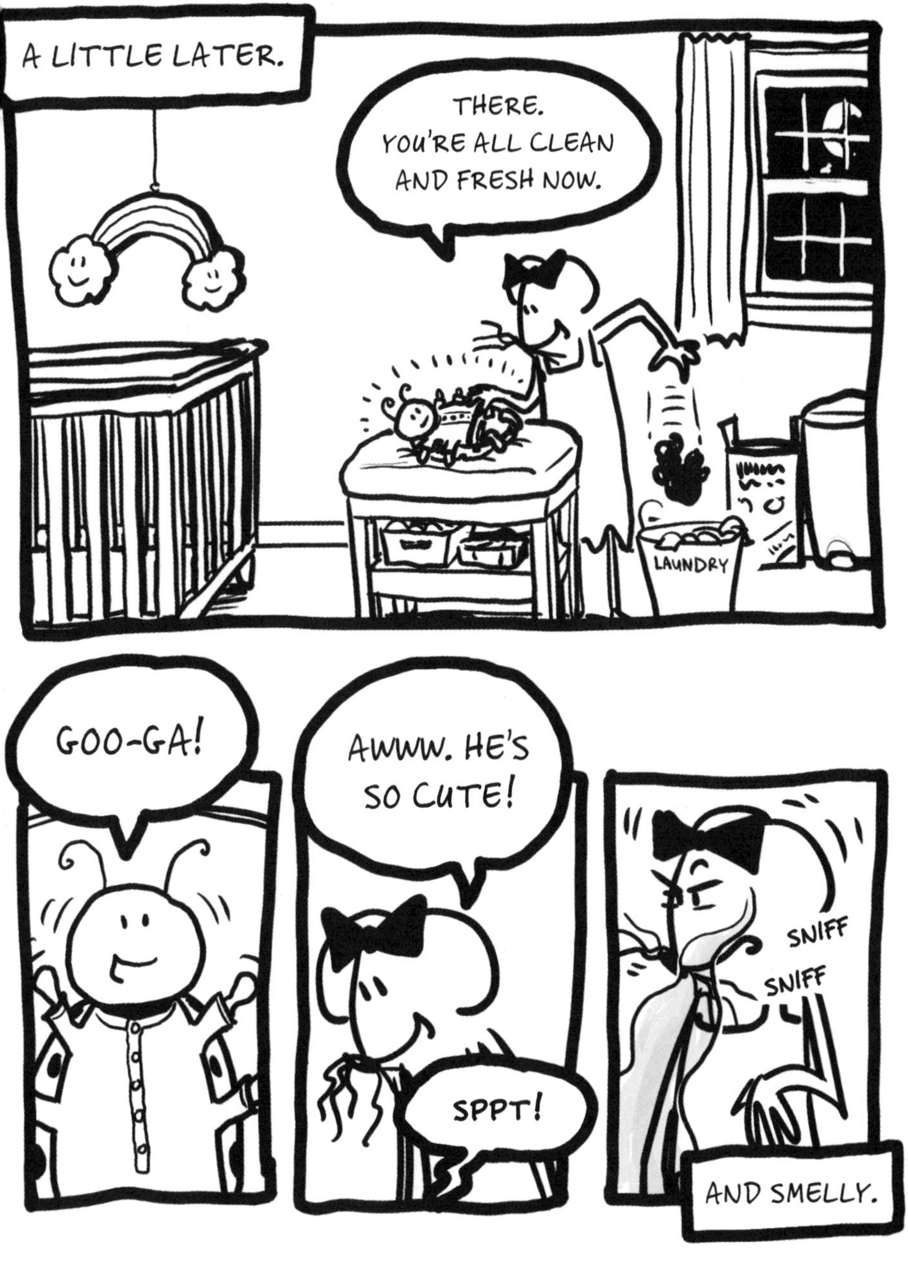
A LITTLE LATER.
THERE. YOU'RE ALL CLEAN AND FRESH NOW.
LAUNDRY
GOO-GA!
AWWW. HE'S SO CUTE!
SPPT!
SNIFF
SNIFF
AND SMELLY.

EWW...

HMM...

DISPOSABLE DIAPERS

SOON.

WET WIPEZ

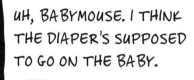

UH, BABYMOUSE. I THINK THE DIAPER'S SUPPOSED TO GO ON THE BABY.

YOU TRY SMELLING THIS, BUSTER.

FWIP!

WET WIPEZ

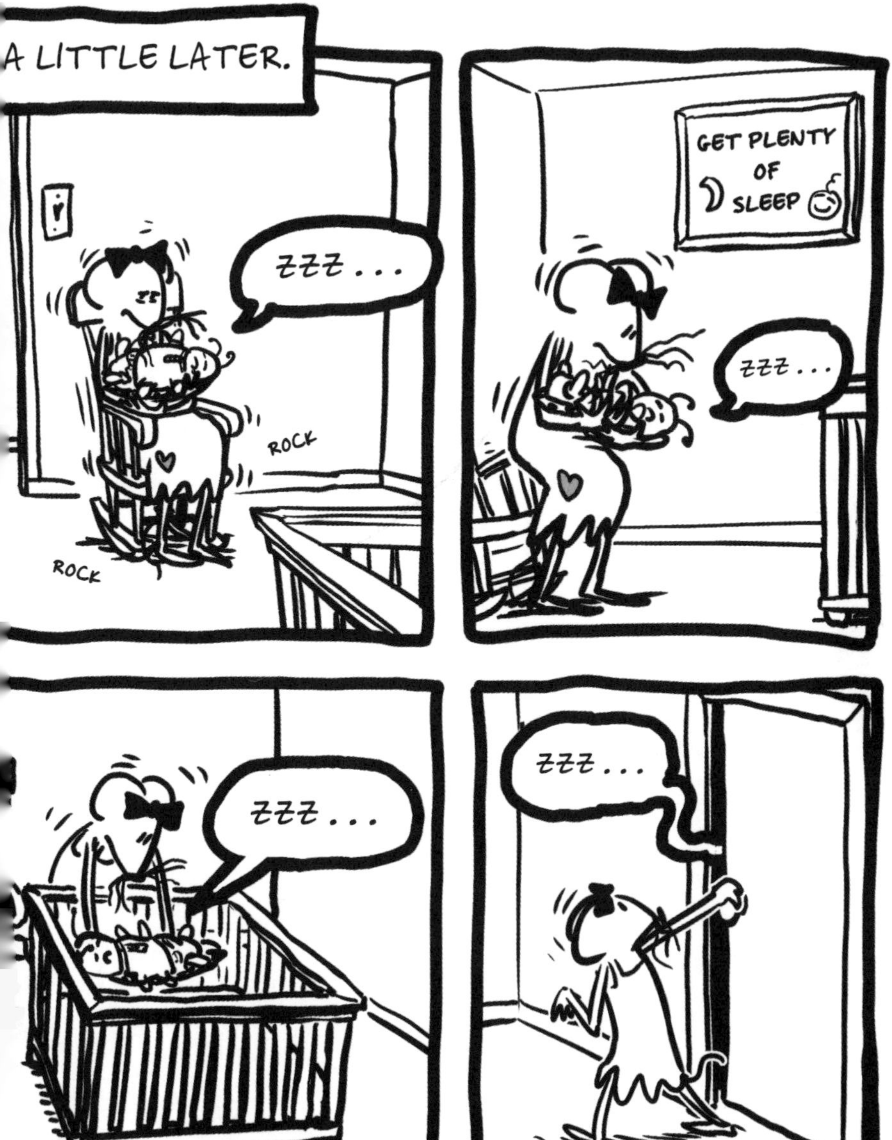
A LITTLE LATER.
ZZZ . . .
ROCK
ROCK
GET PLENTY OF SLEEP
ZZZ . . .
ZZZ . . .
ZZZ . . .

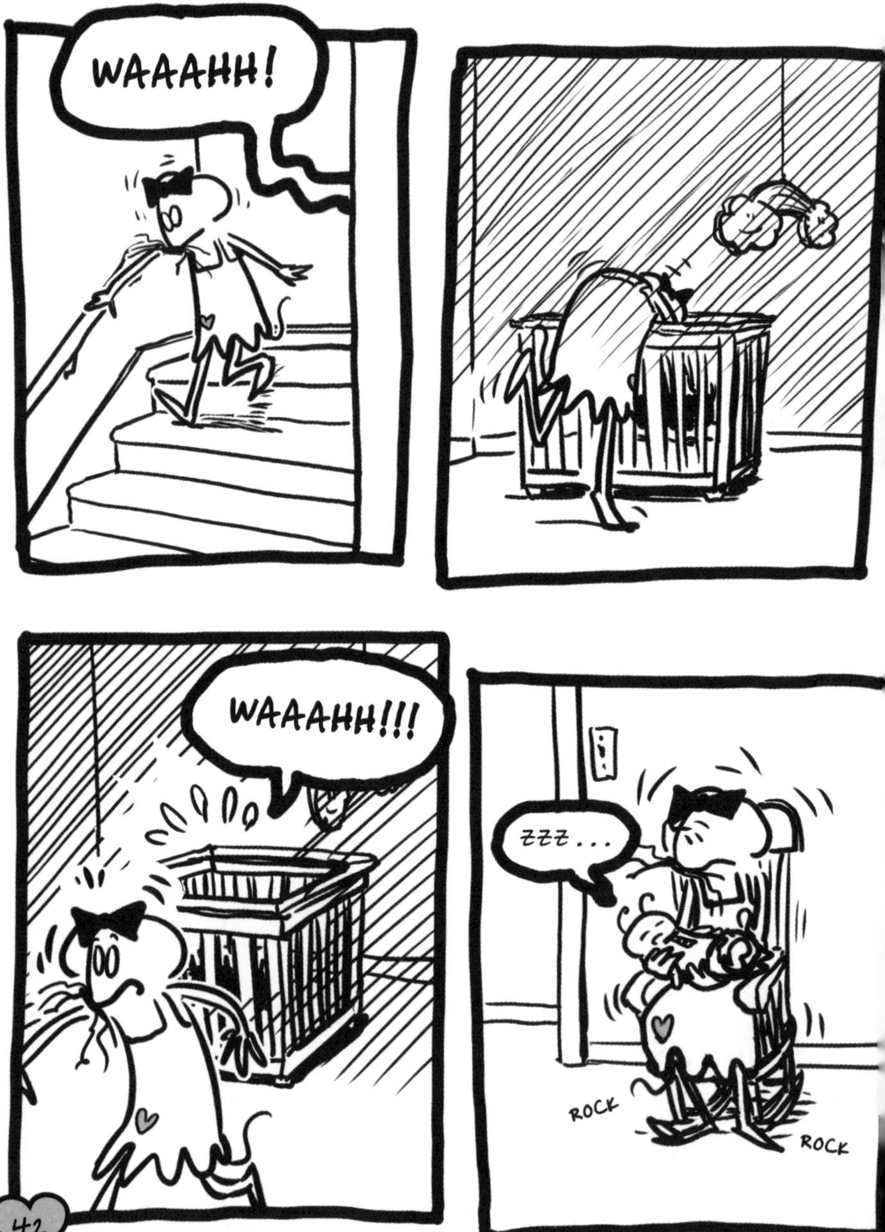
WAAAHH!
WAAAHH!!!
ZZZ...
ROCK
ROCK

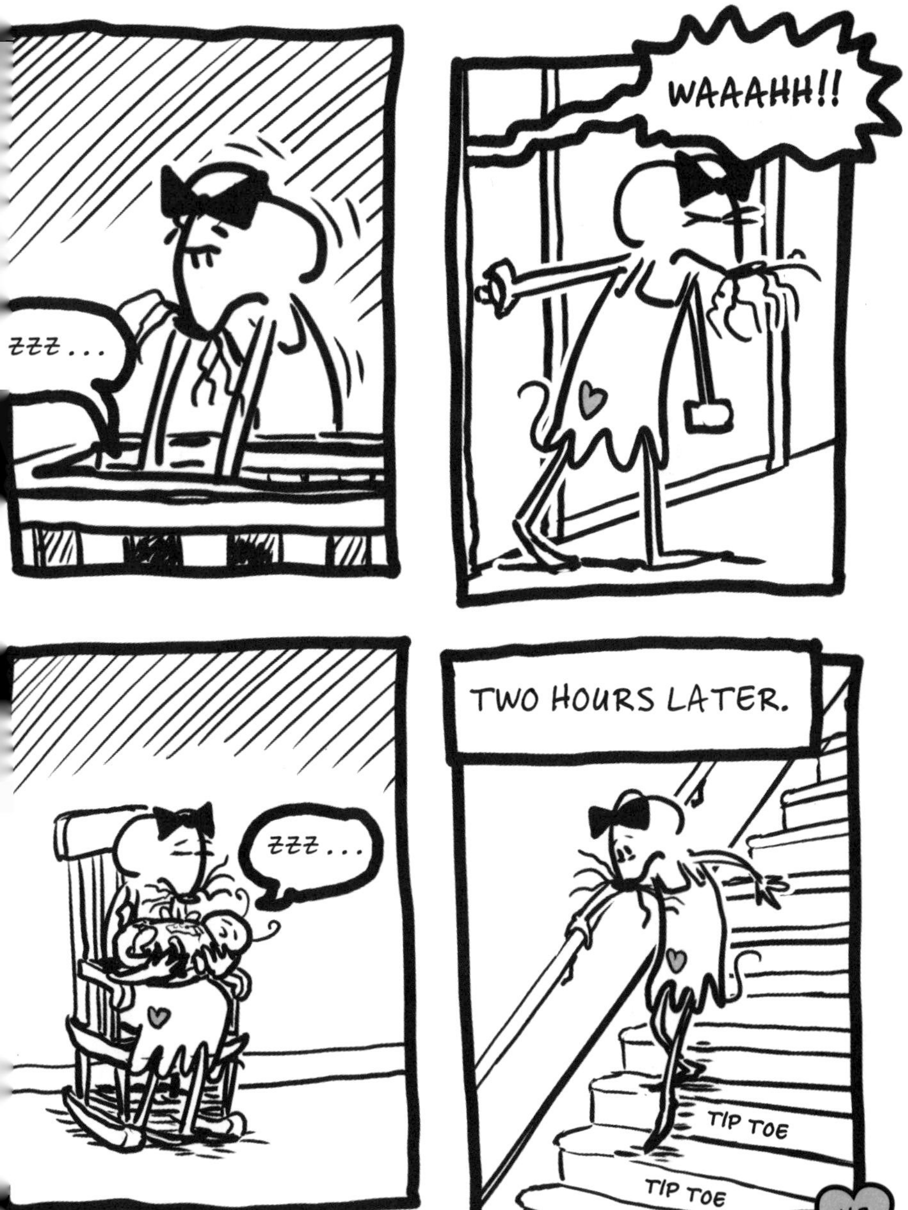

ZZZ . . .
WAAAHH!!
ZZZ . . .
TWO HOURS LATER.
TIP TOE
TIP TOE

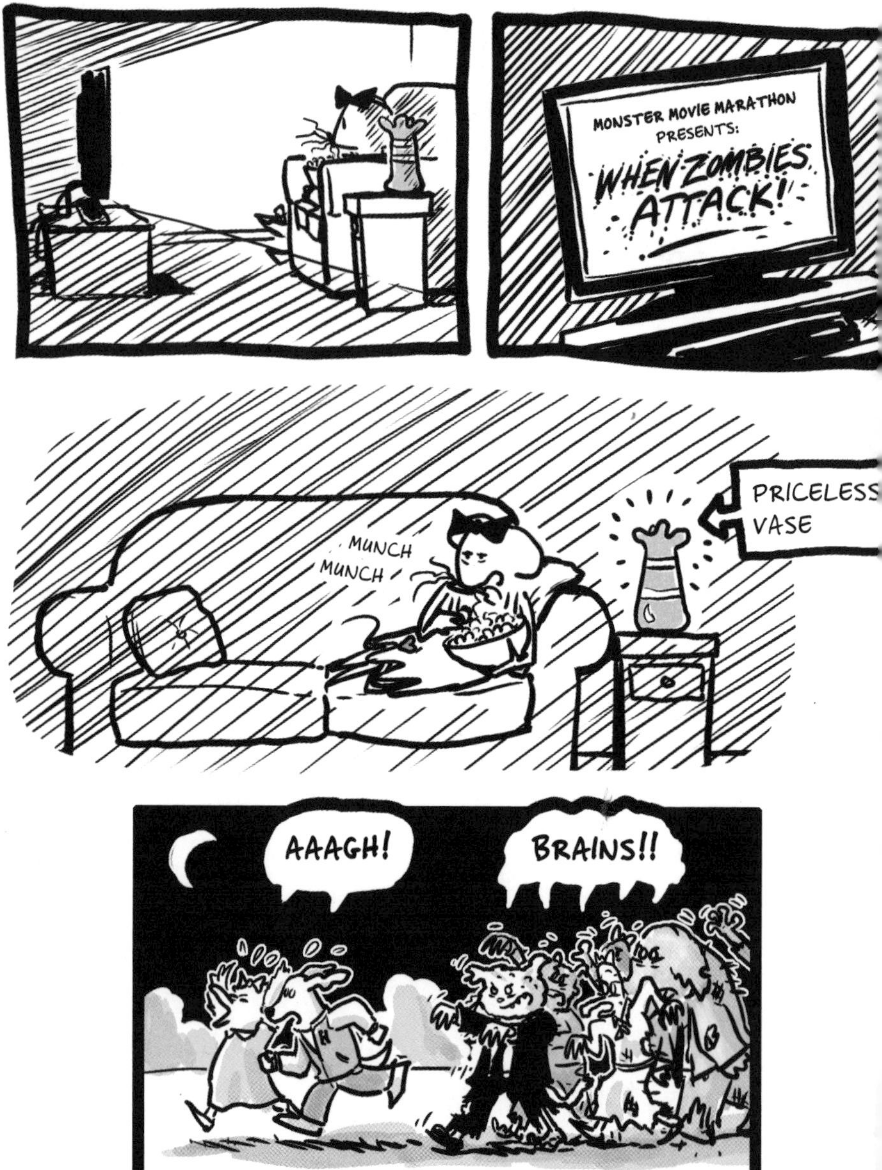
MONSTER MOVIE MARATHON
PRESENTS:
WHEN ZOMBIES ATTACK!
MUNCH
MUNCH
PRICELESS VASE
AAAGH!
BRAINS!!

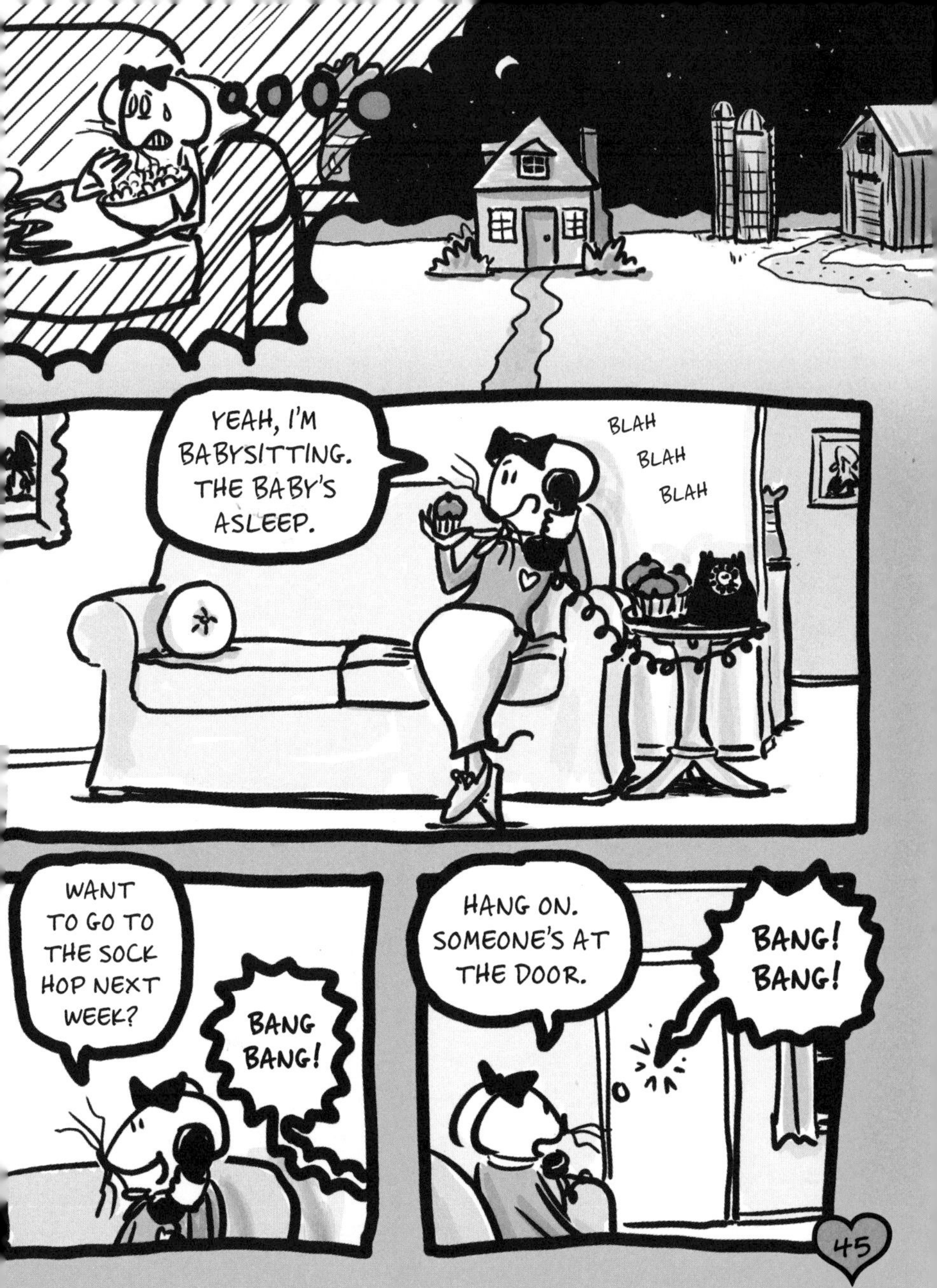
YEAH, I'M BABYSITTING. THE BABY'S ASLEEP.
BLAH BLAH BLAH
WANT TO GO TO THE SOCK HOP NEXT WEEK?
BANG BANG!
HANG ON. SOMEONE'S AT THE DOOR.
BANG! BANG!

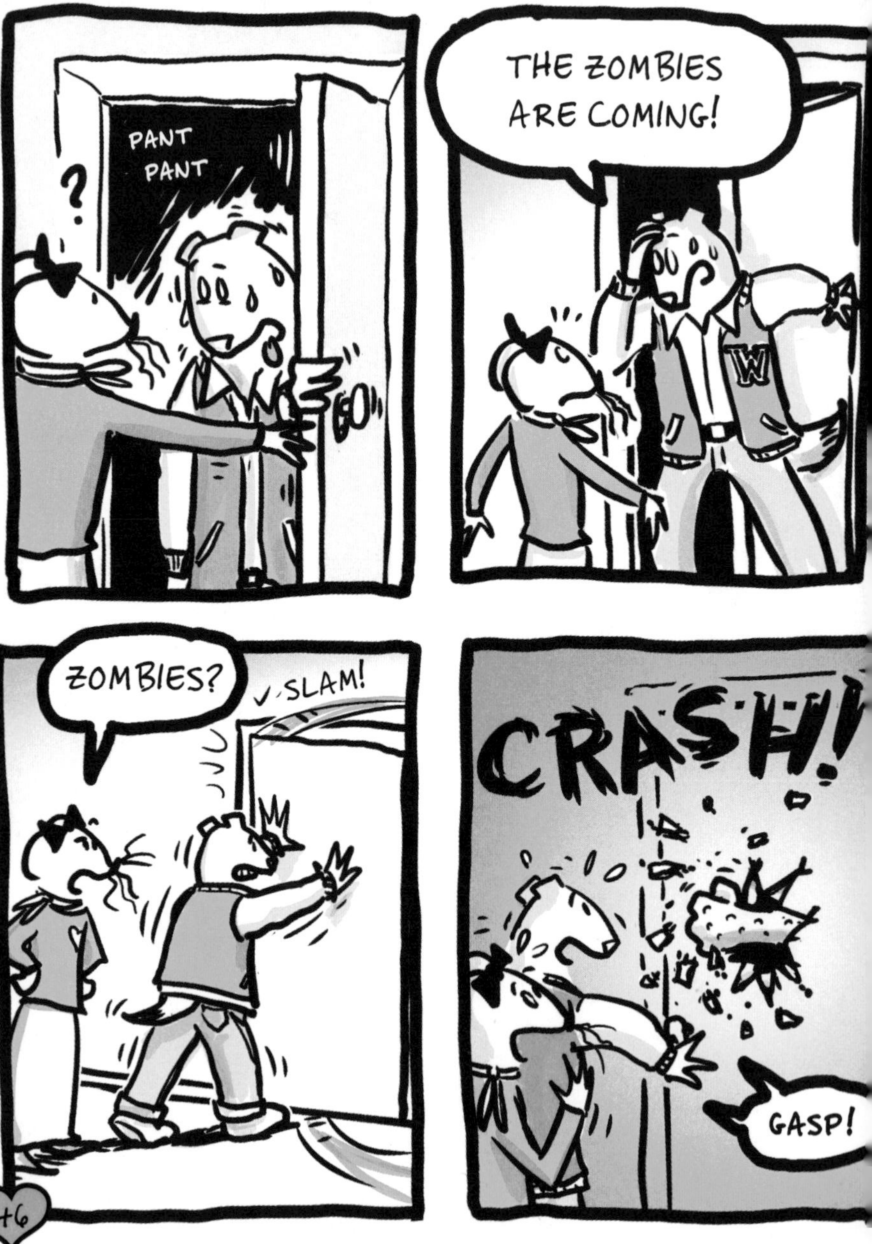
PANT
PANT
?
THE ZOMBIES ARE COMING!
W
ZOMBIES?
SLAM!
CRASH!
GASP!

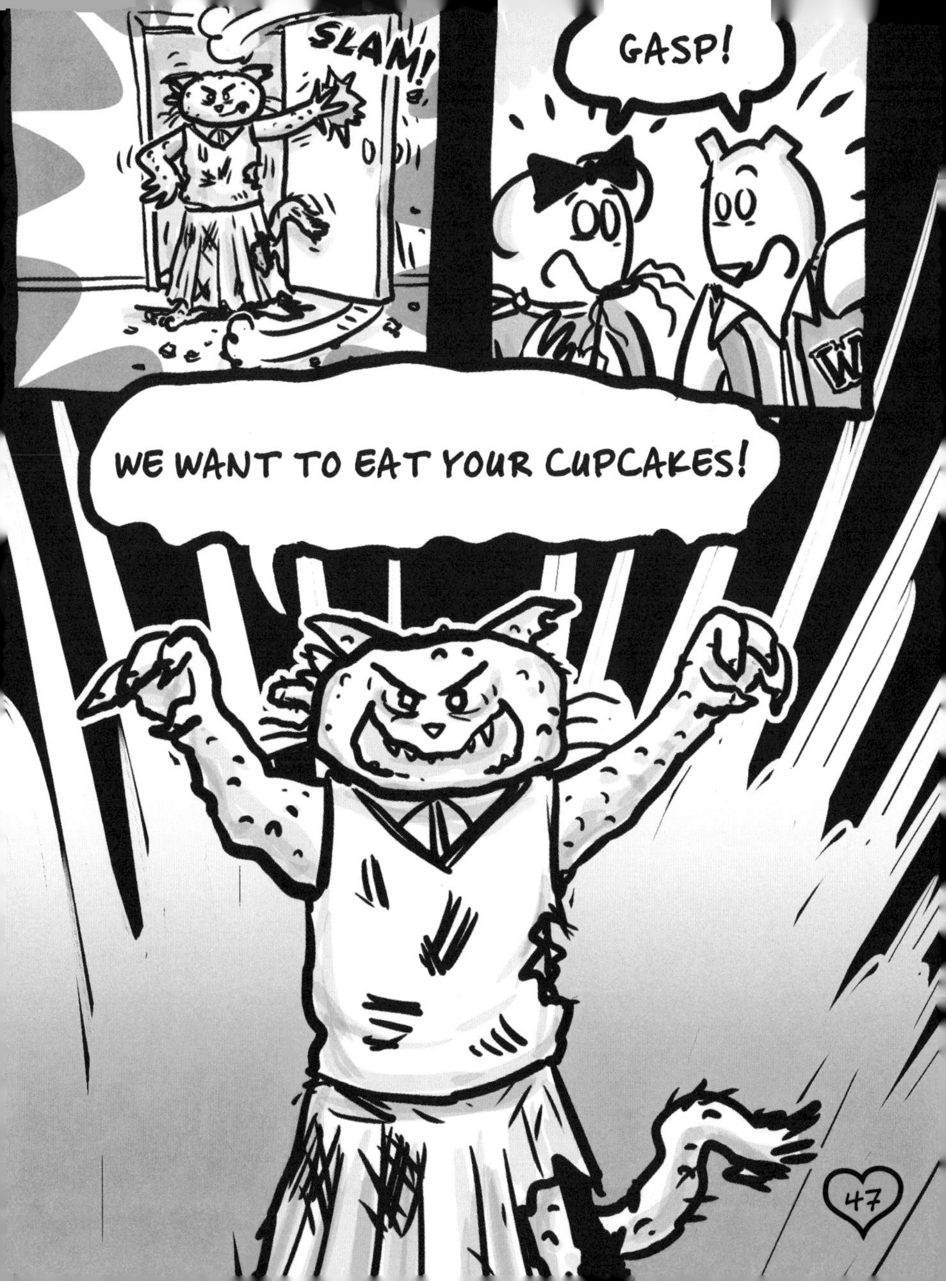
SLAM!
GASP!
WE WANT TO EAT YOUR CUPCAKES!

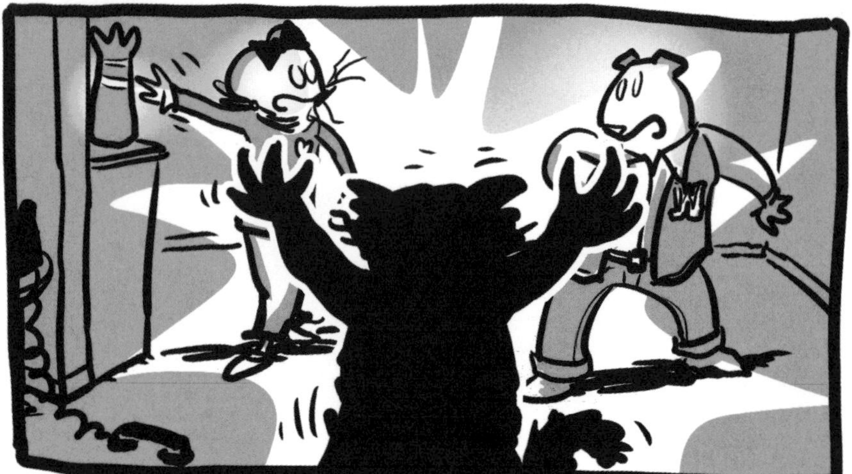

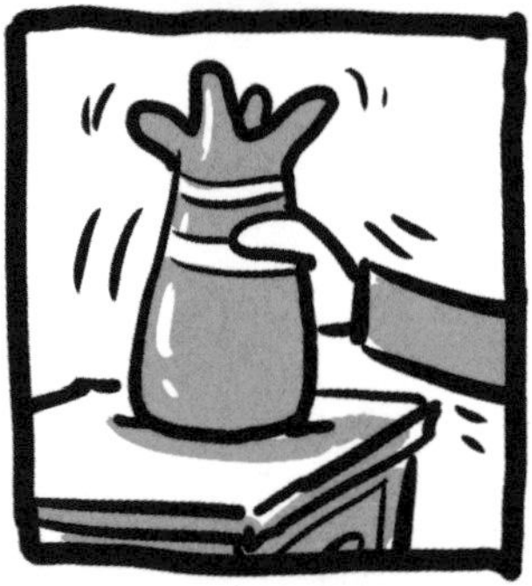

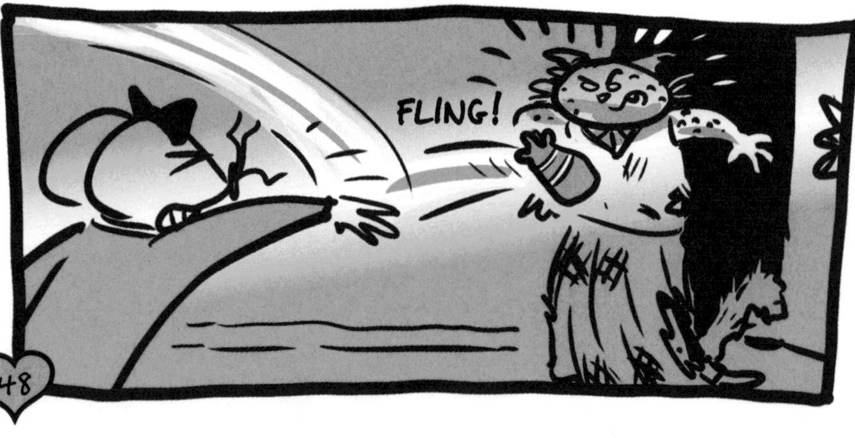
FLING!

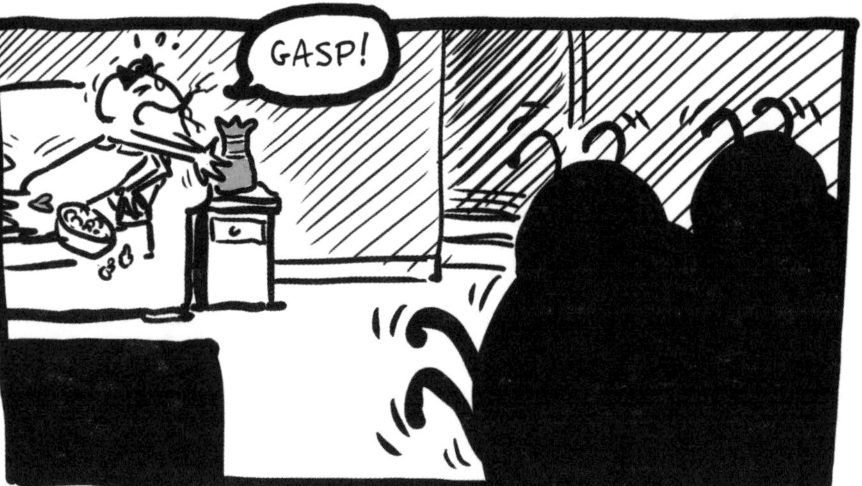
GASP!

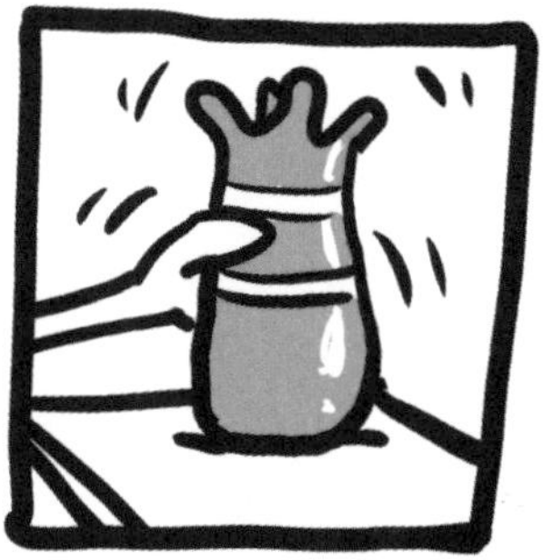

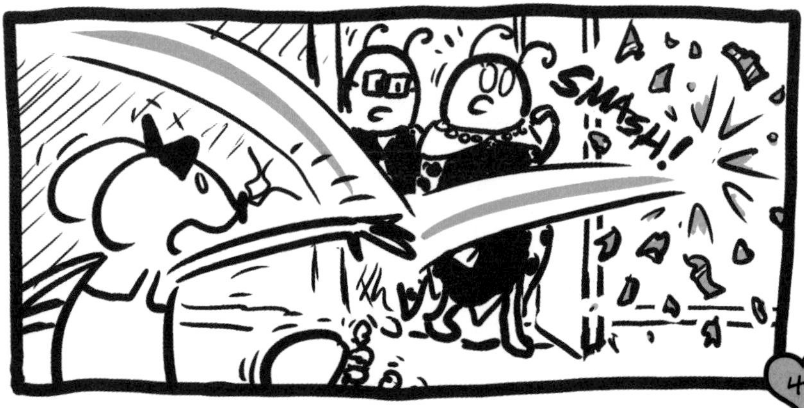
SMASH!

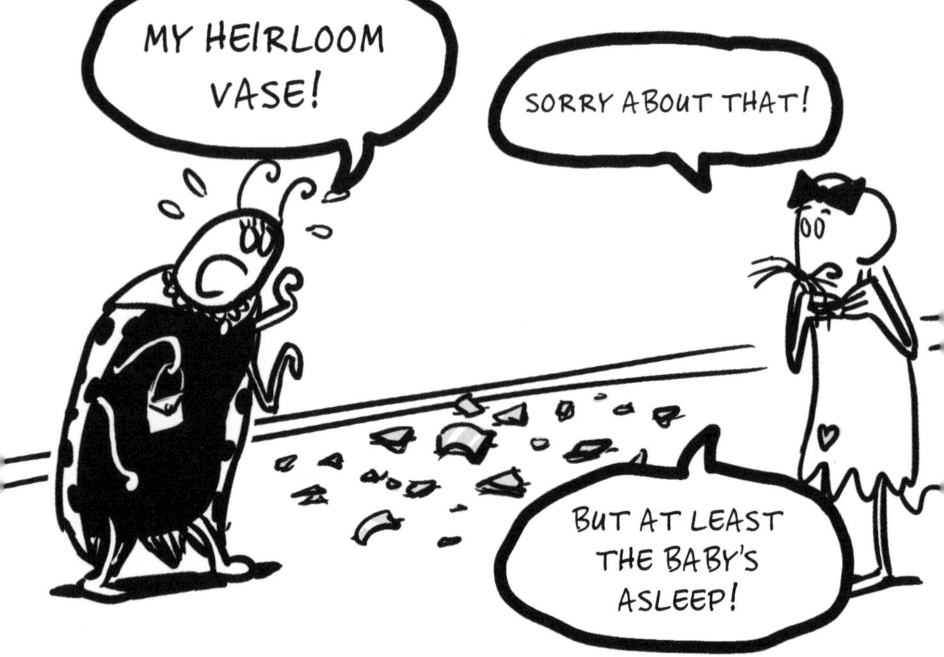
MY HEIRLOOM VASE!
SORRY ABOUT THAT!
BUT AT LEAST THE BABY'S ASLEEP!

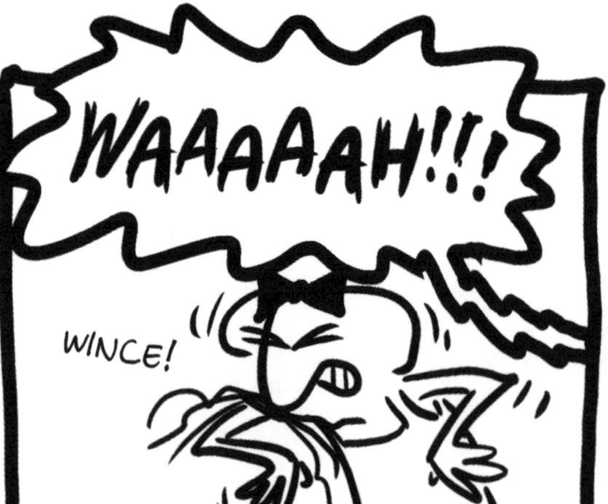
WAAAAAH!!!
WINCE!

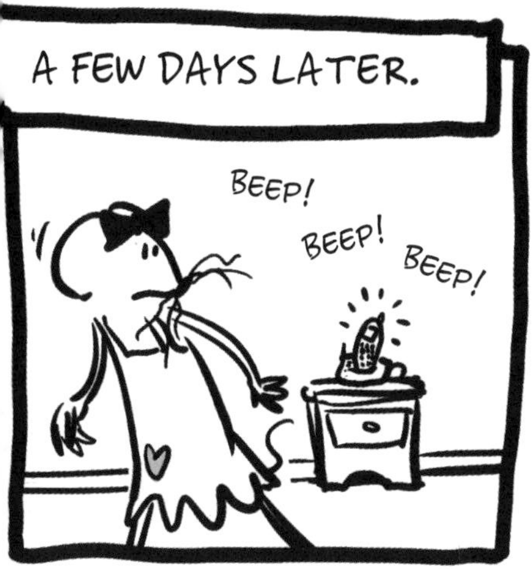
A FEW DAYS LATER.
BEEP!
BEEP!
BEEP!

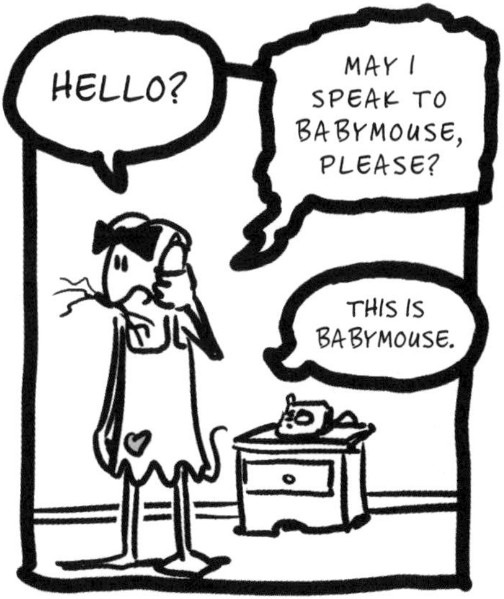
HELLO?
MAY I SPEAK TO BABYMOUSE, PLEASE?
THIS IS BABYMOUSE.

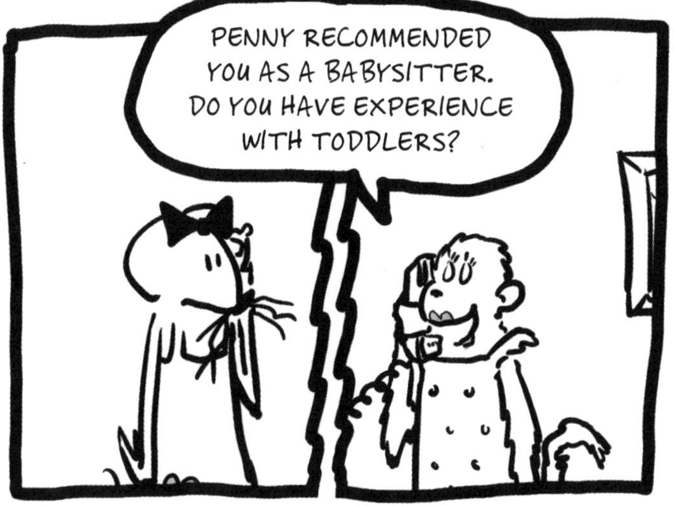
PENNY RECOMMENDED YOU AS A BABYSITTER. DO YOU HAVE EXPERIENCE WITH TODDLERS?

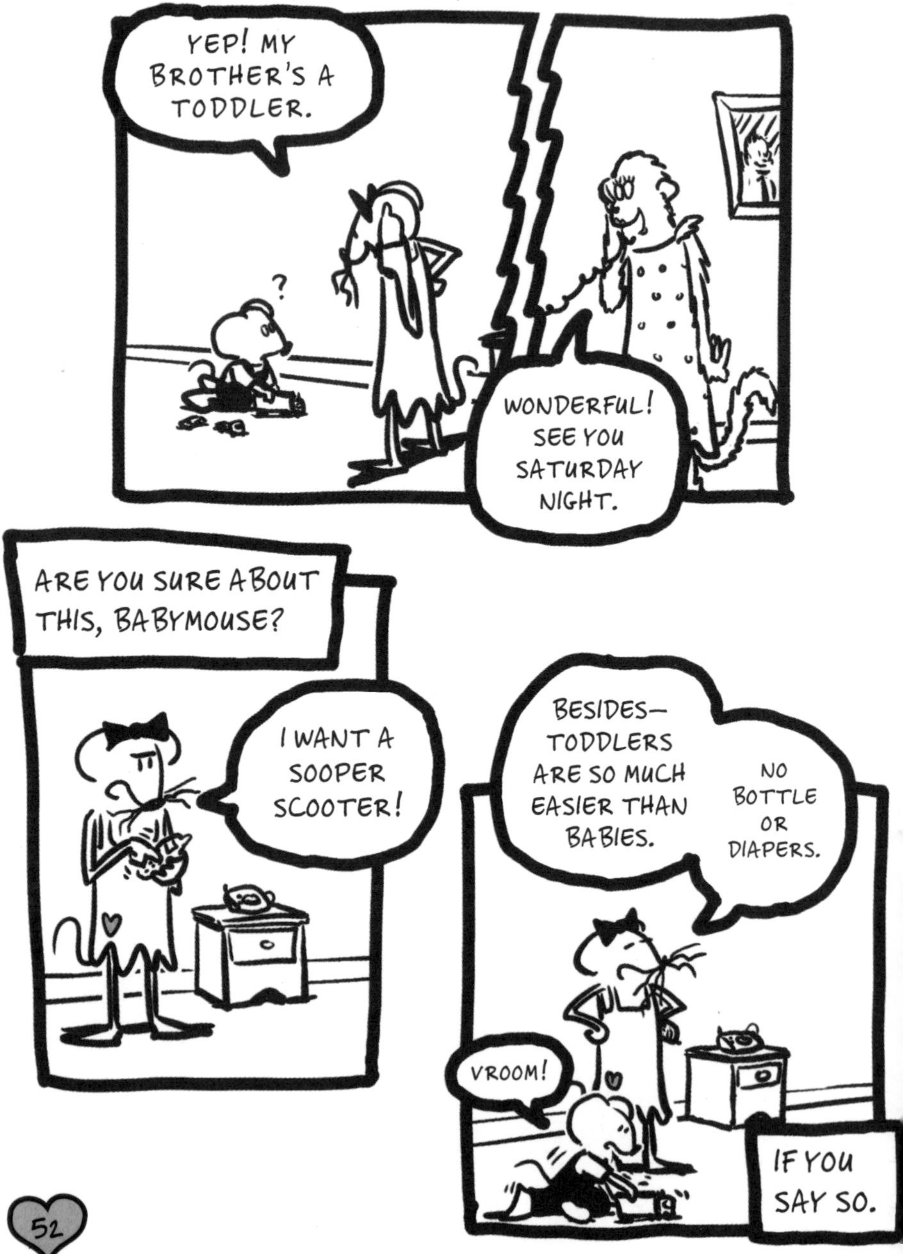

YEP! MY BROTHER'S A TODDLER.
?
WONDERFUL! SEE YOU SATURDAY NIGHT.
ARE YOU SURE ABOUT THIS, BABYMOUSE?
I WANT A SOOPER SCOOTER!
BESIDES— TODDLERS ARE SO MUCH EASIER THAN BABIES.
NO BOTTLE OR DIAPERS.
VROOM!
IF YOU SAY SO.

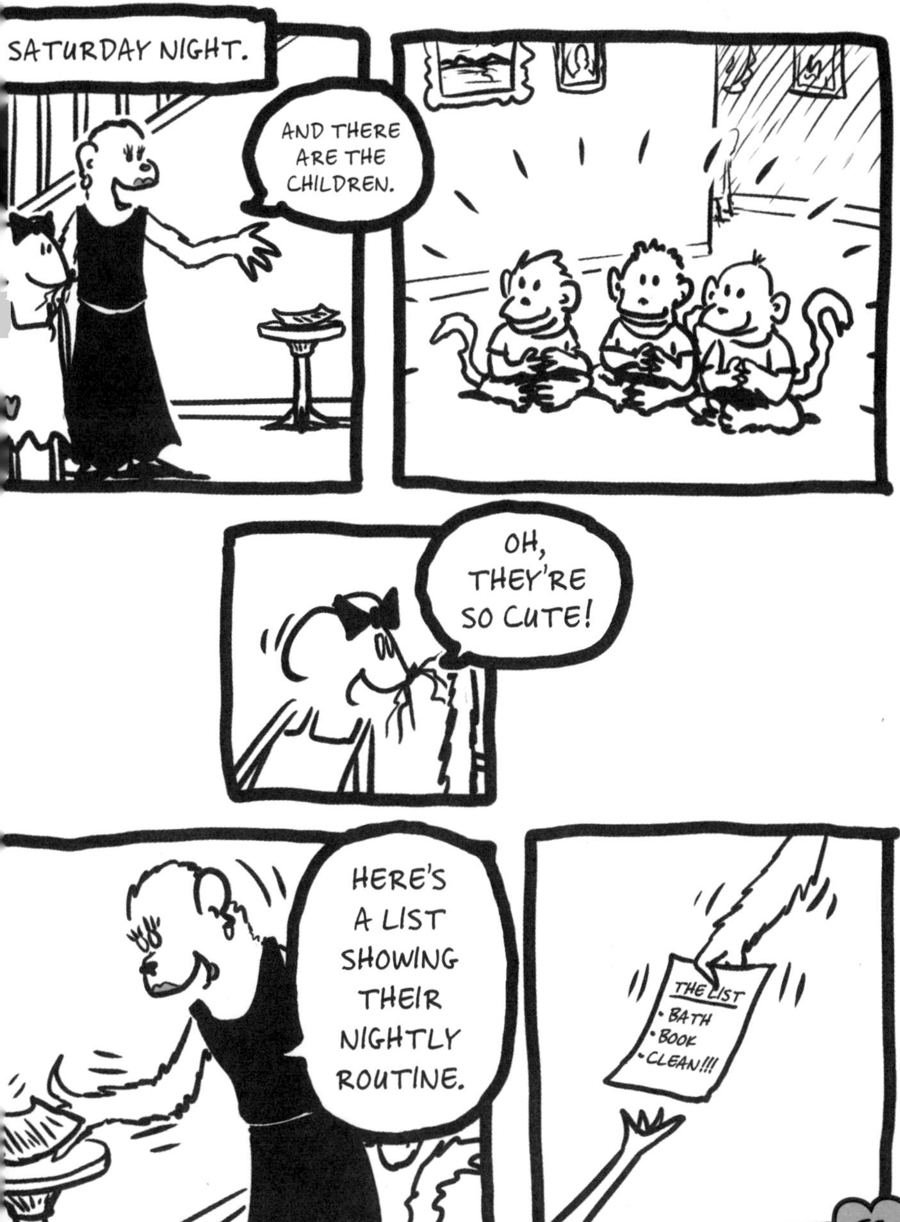
SATURDAY NIGHT.
AND THERE ARE THE CHILDREN.
OH, THEY'RE SO CUTE!
HERE'S A LIST SHOWING THEIR NIGHTLY ROUTINE.
THE LIST
• BATH
• BOOK
• CLEAN!!!

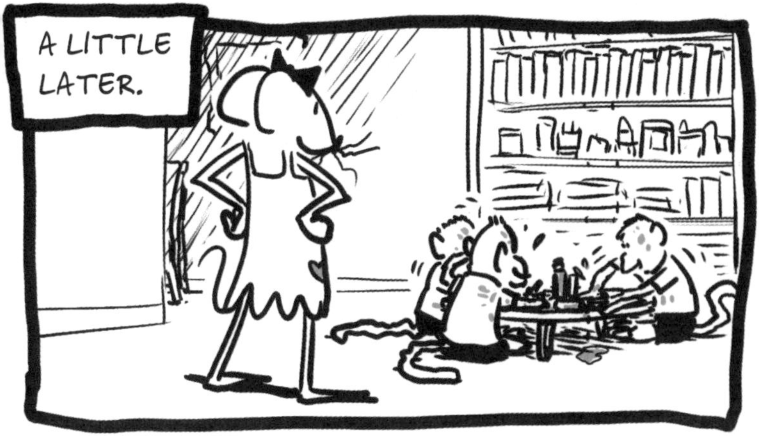
A LITTLE LATER.

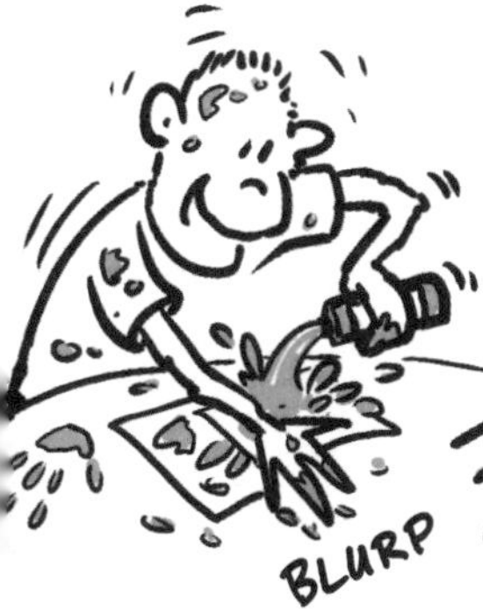
BLURP

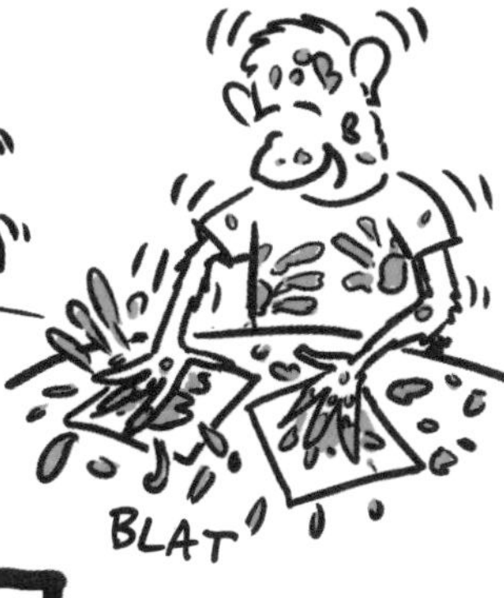
BLAT

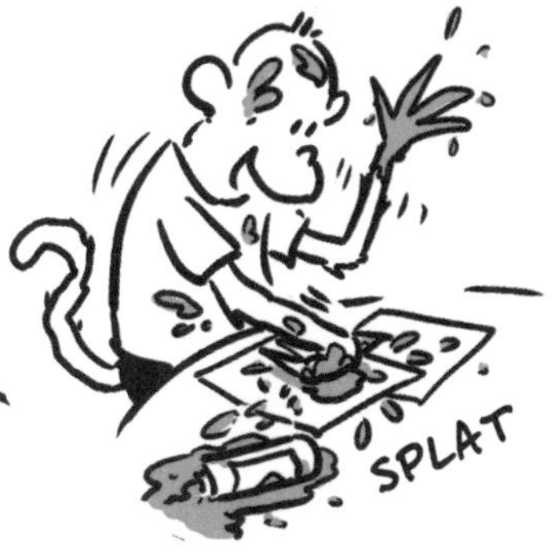
SPLAT

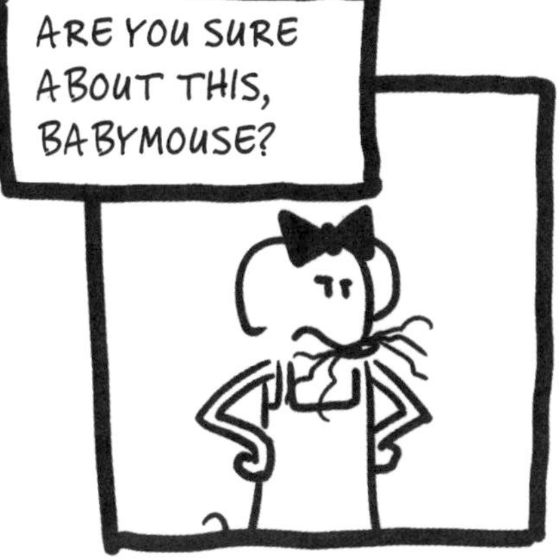
ARE YOU SURE ABOUT THIS, BABYMOUSE?

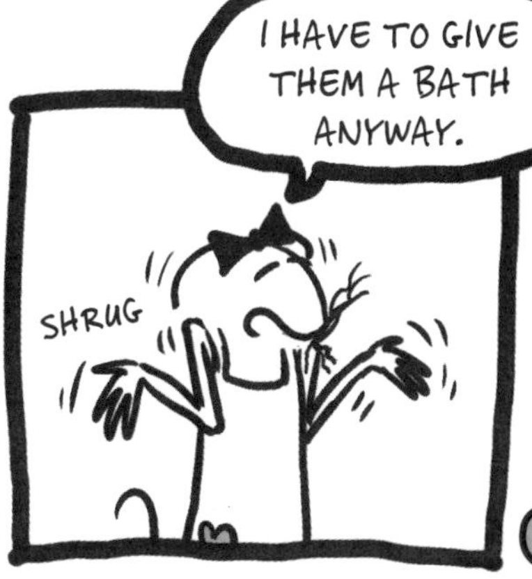
I HAVE TO GIVE THEM A BATH ANYWAY.
SHRUG

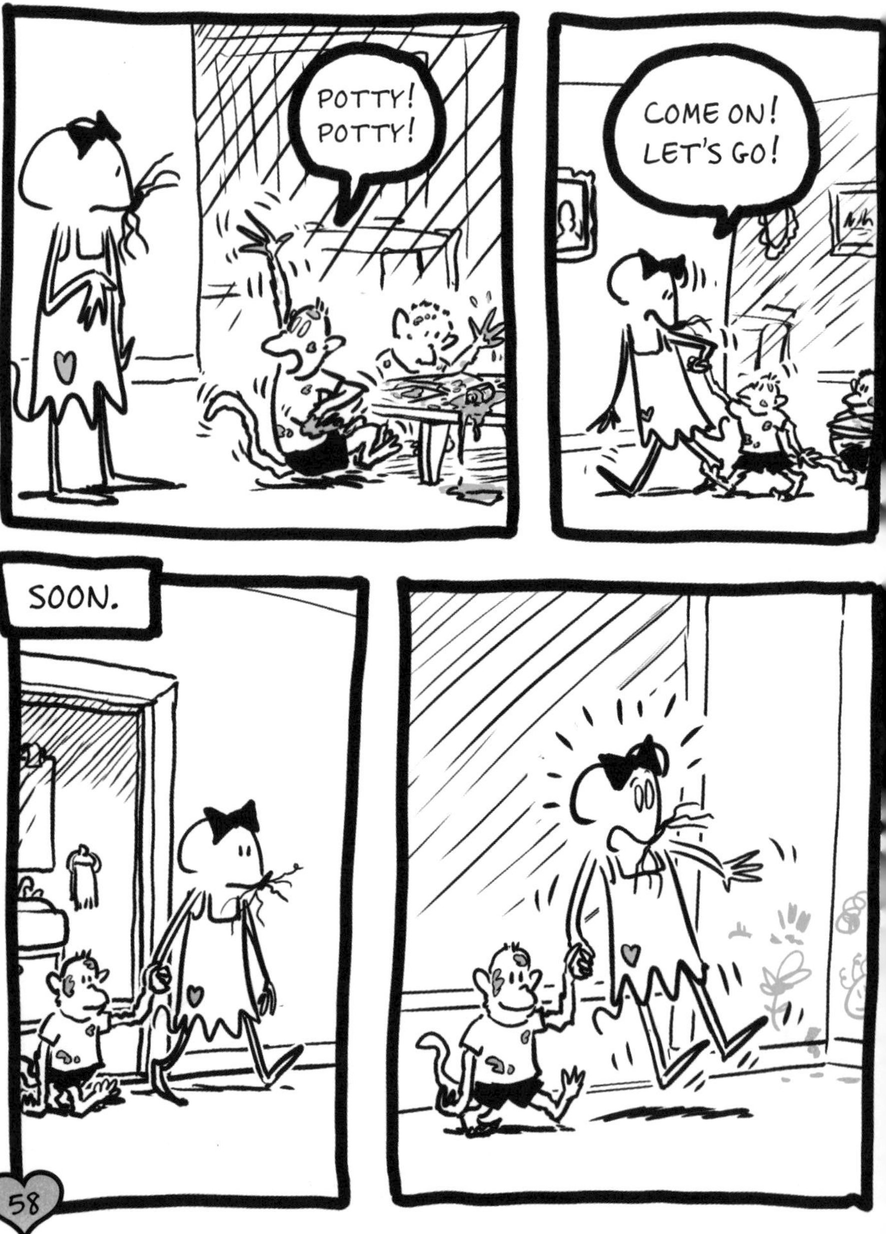
POTTY! POTTY!
COME ON! LET'S GO!
SOON.

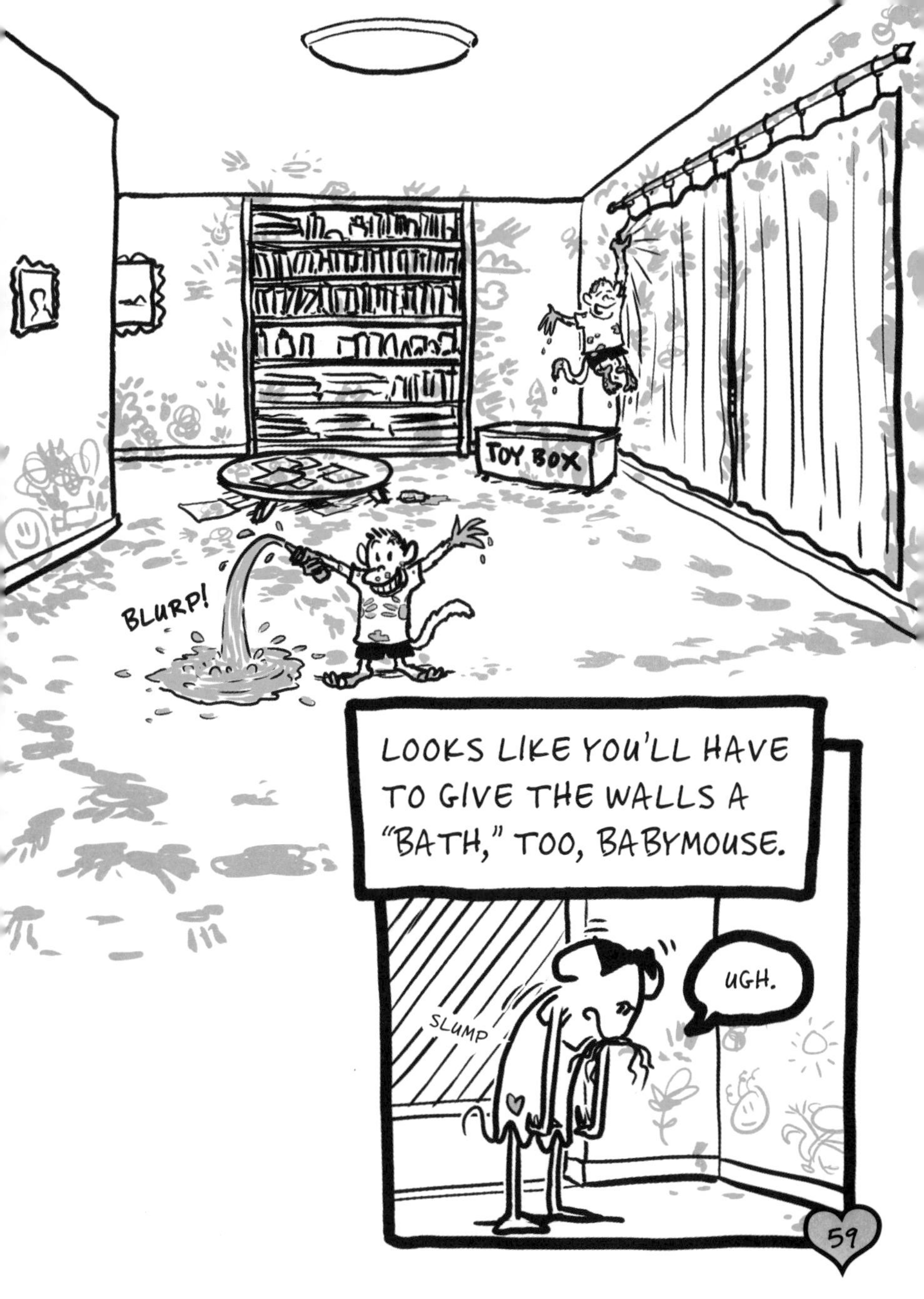
TOY BOX
BLURP!
LOOKS LIKE YOU'LL HAVE TO GIVE THE WALLS A "BATH," TOO, BABYMOUSE.
SLUMP
UGH.

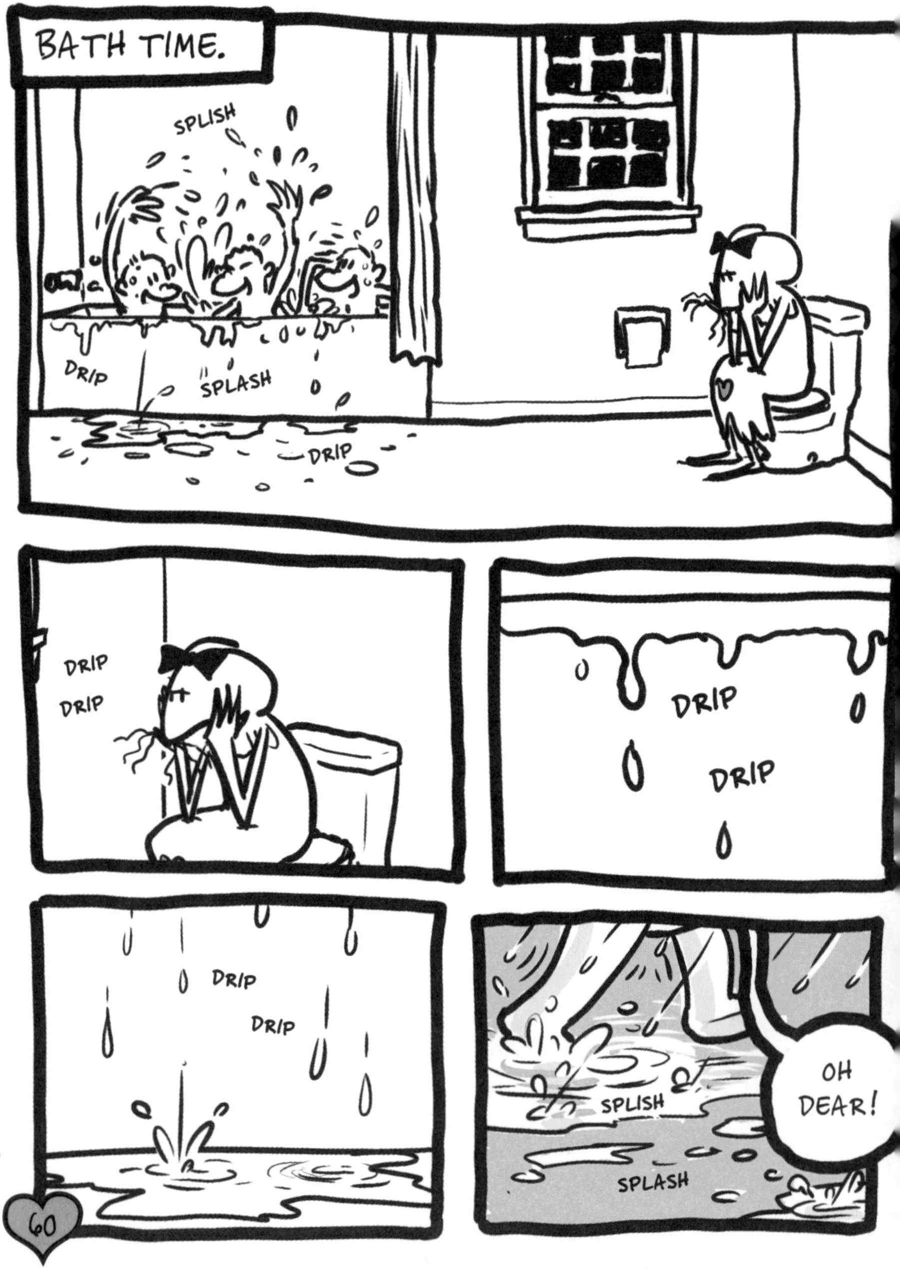
BATH TIME.
SPLISH
DRIP
SPLASH
DRIP
DRIP
DRIP
DRIP
DRIP
DRIP
DRIP
SPLISH
SPLASH
OH DEAR!

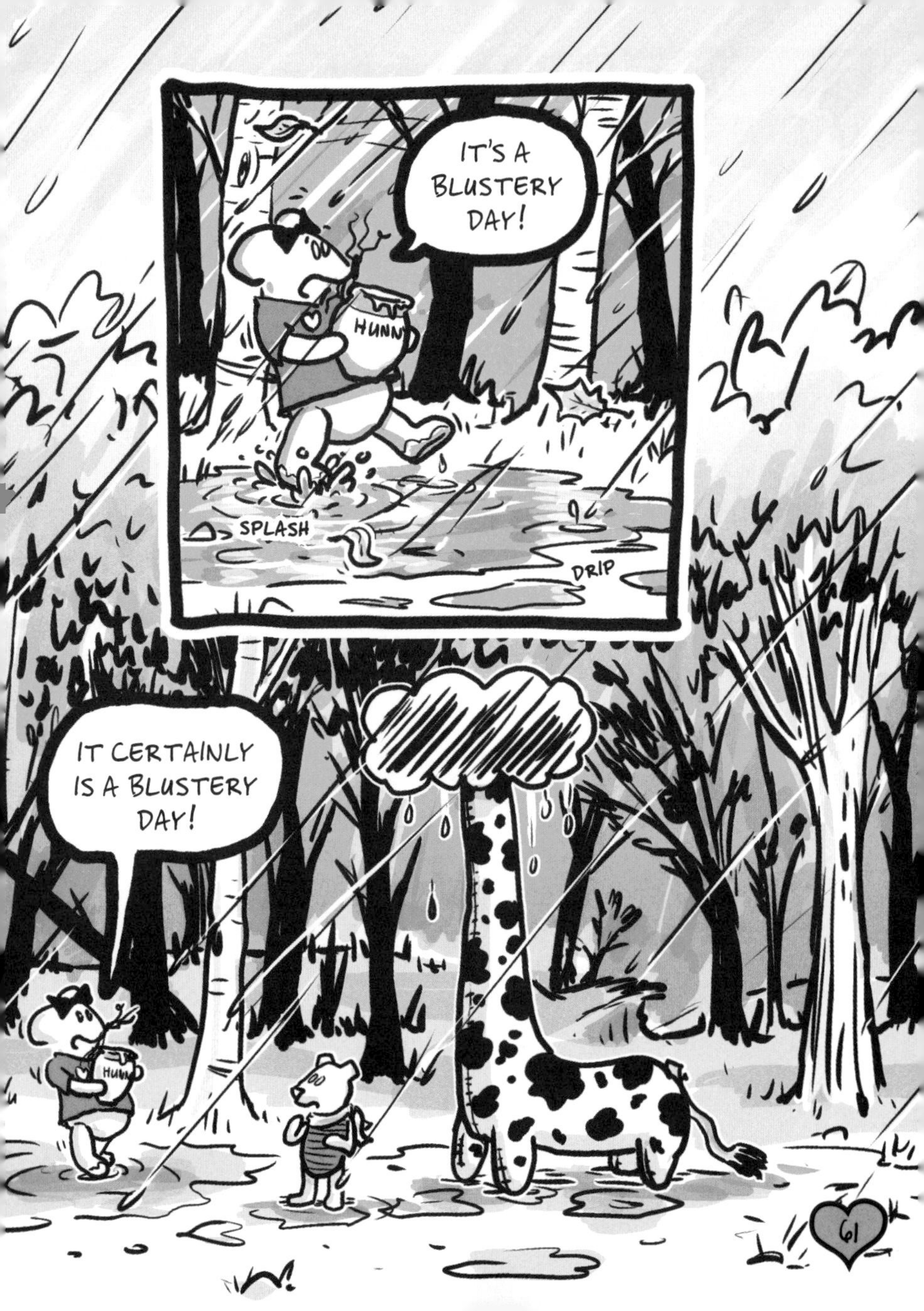
IT'S A BLUSTERY DAY!
HUNN
SPLASH
DRIP
IT CERTAINLY IS A BLUSTERY DAY!
HUNN

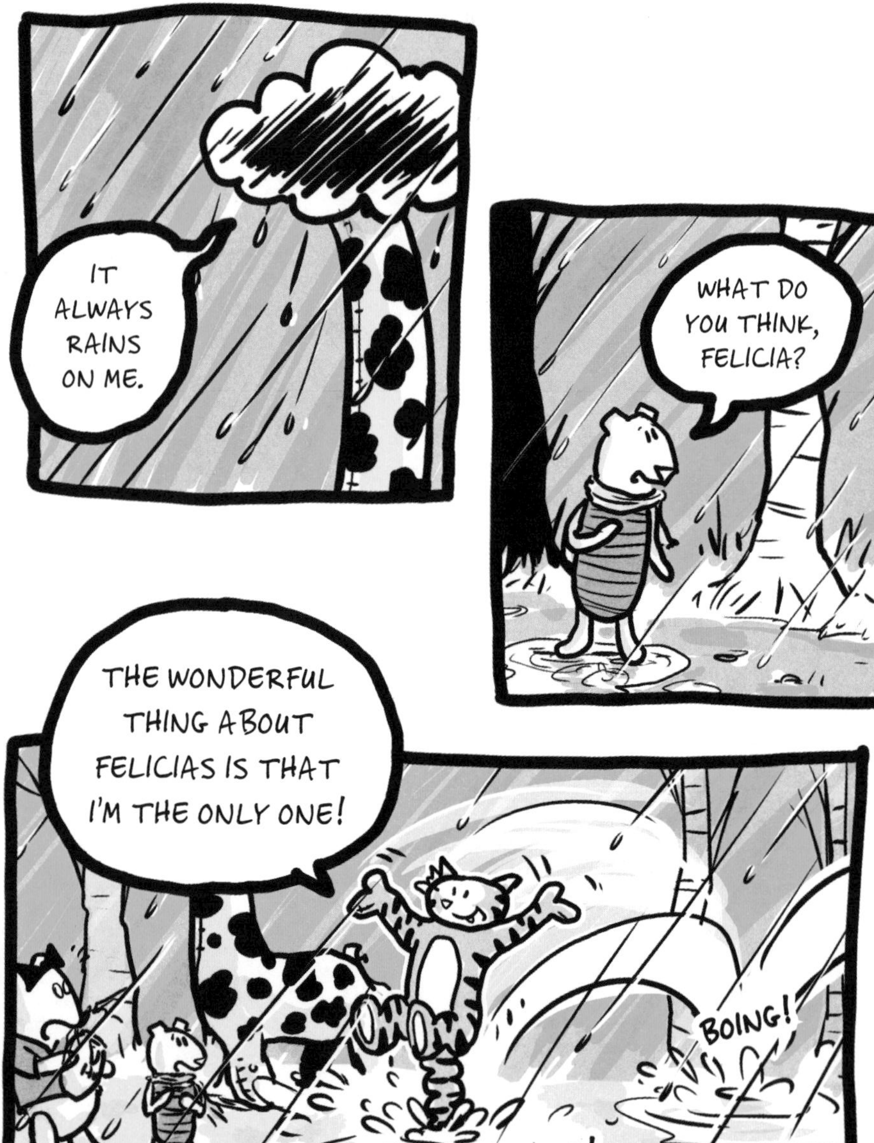
IT ALWAYS RAINS ON ME.
WHAT DO YOU THINK, FELICIA?
THE WONDERFUL THING ABOUT FELICIAS IS THAT I'M THE ONLY ONE!
SPLASH!
BOING!
BOING!

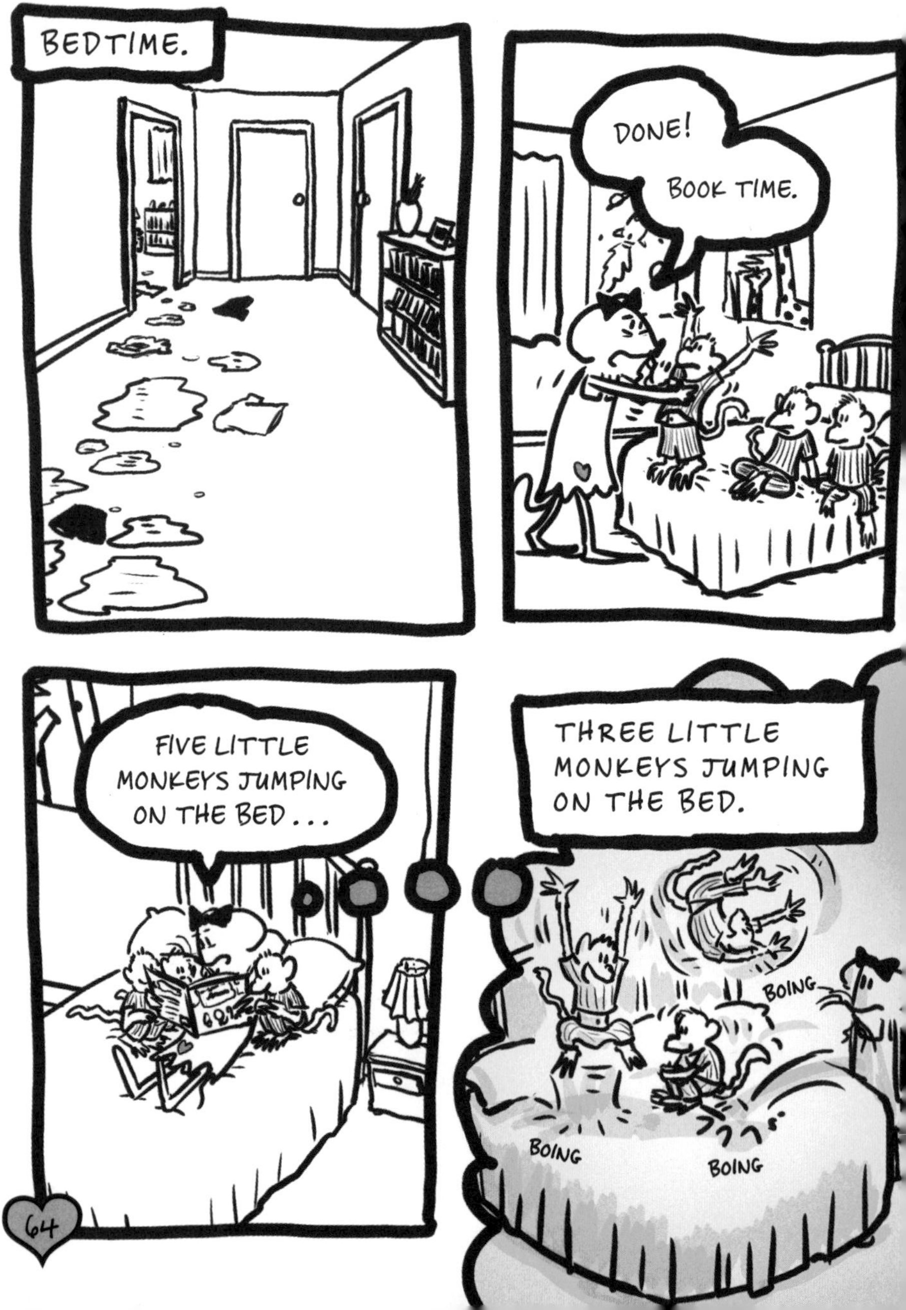
BEDTIME.
DONE!
BOOK TIME.
FIVE LITTLE MONKEYS JUMPING ON THE BED . . .
THREE LITTLE MONKEYS JUMPING ON THE BED.
BOING
BOING
BOING

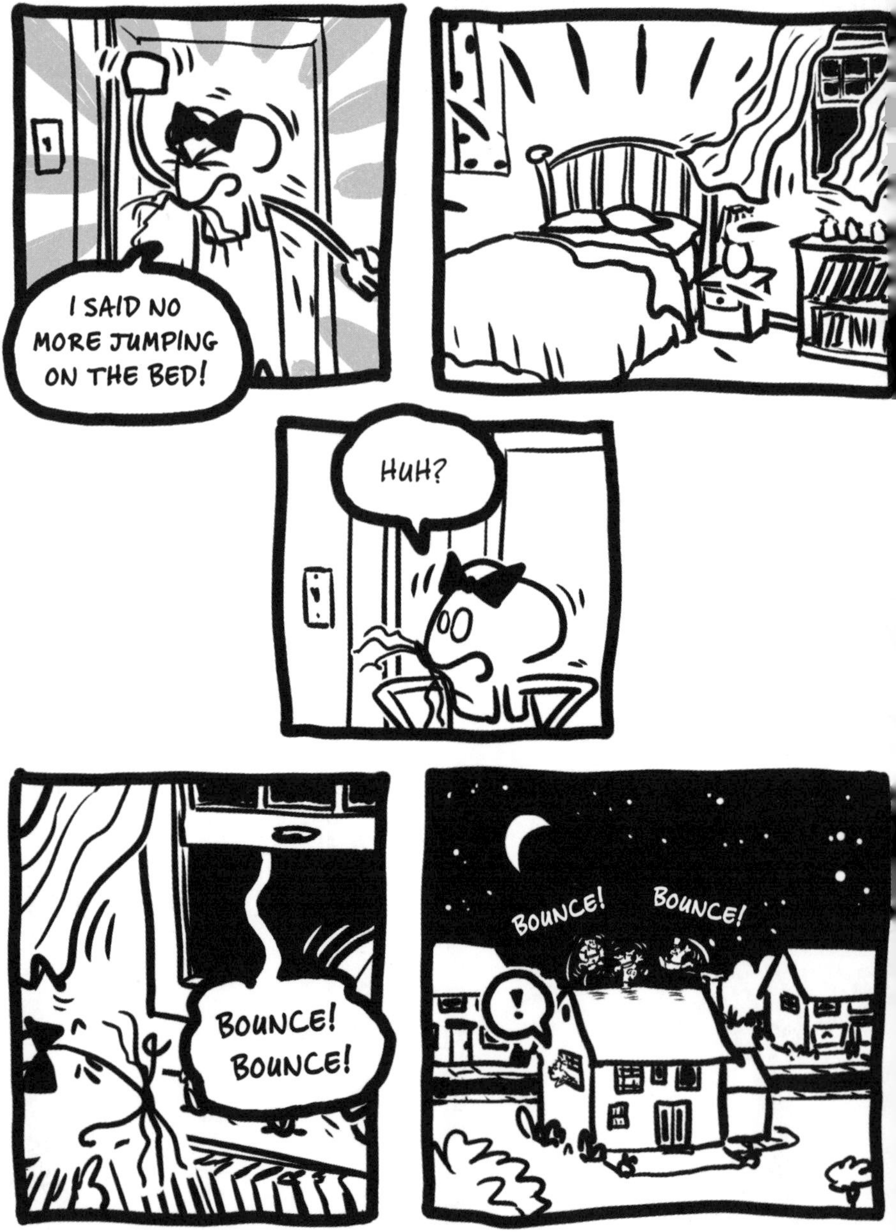
I SAID NO MORE JUMPING ON THE BED!
HUH?
BOUNCE! BOUNCE!
BOUNCE!
BOUNCE!
!

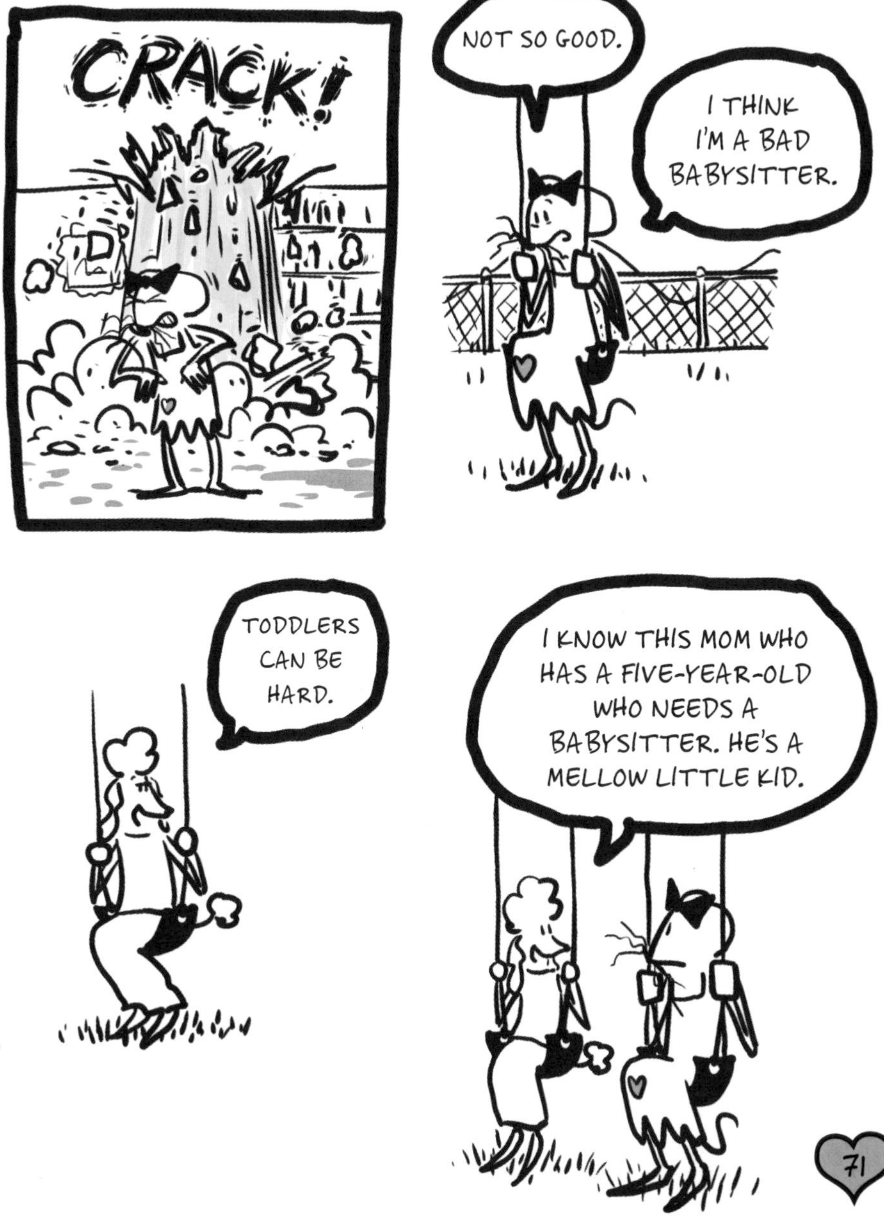
CRACK!
NOT SO GOOD.
I THINK I'M A BAD BABYSITTER.
TODDLERS CAN BE HARD.
I KNOW THIS MOM WHO HAS A FIVE-YEAR-OLD WHO NEEDS A BABYSITTER. HE'S A MELLOW LITTLE KID.

HI! I'M BABYMOUSE.
YOUR NEW BABYSITTER.

NOD

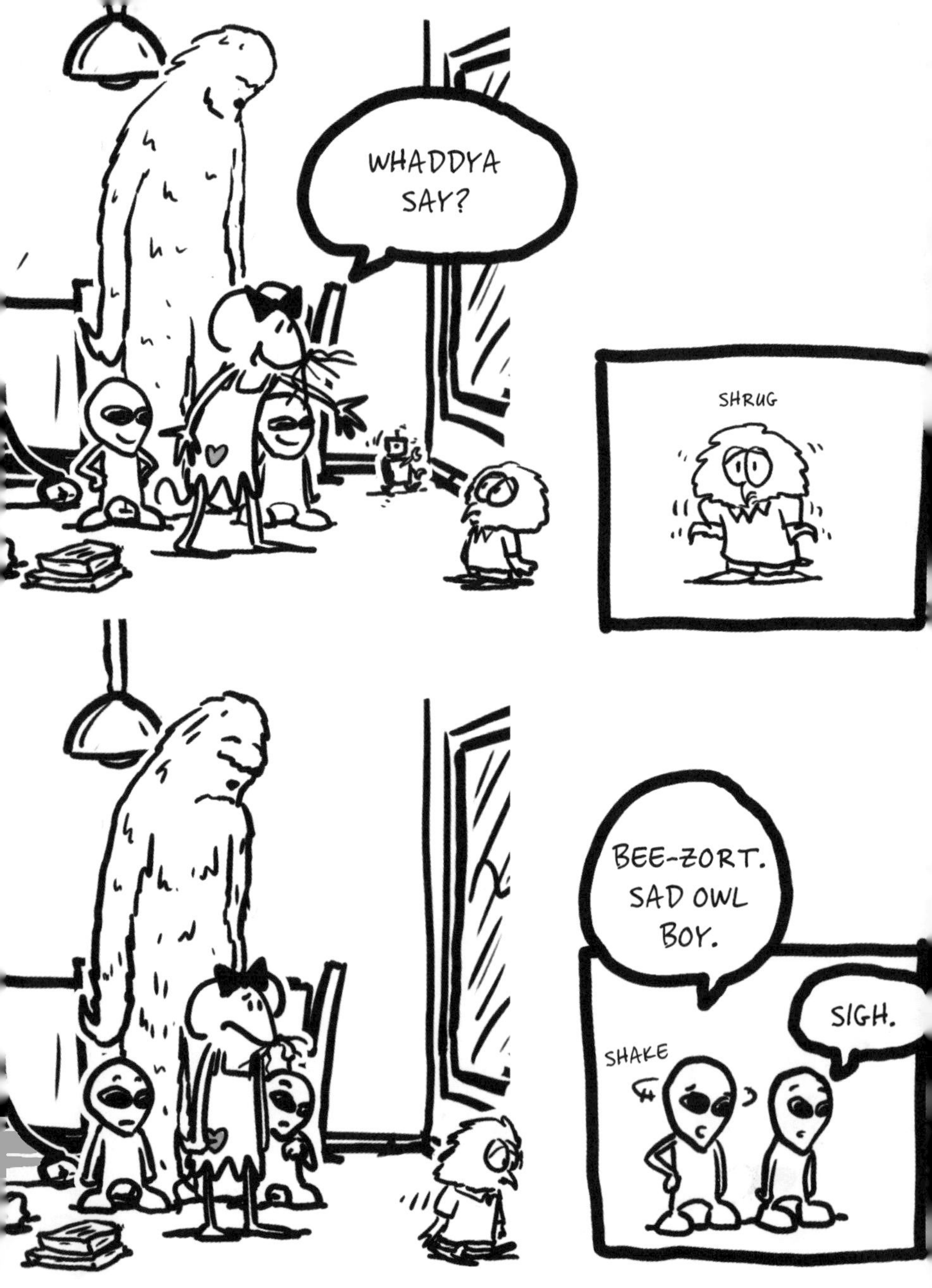
WHADDYA SAY?
SHRUG
BEE-ZORT. SAD OWL BOY.
SHAKE
SIGH.

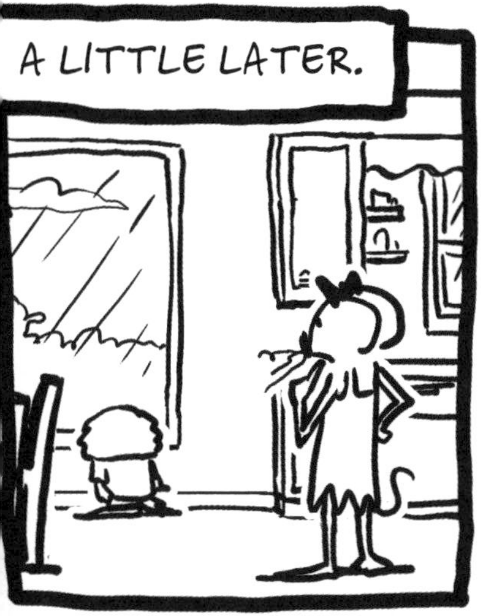
A LITTLE LATER.

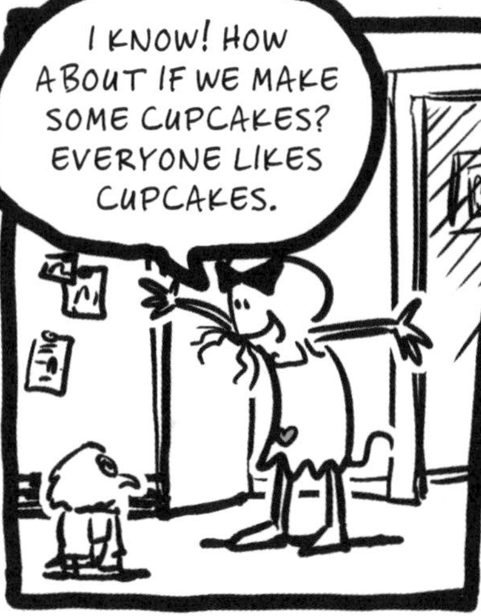
I KNOW! HOW ABOUT IF WE MAKE SOME CUPCAKES? EVERYONE LIKES CUPCAKES.

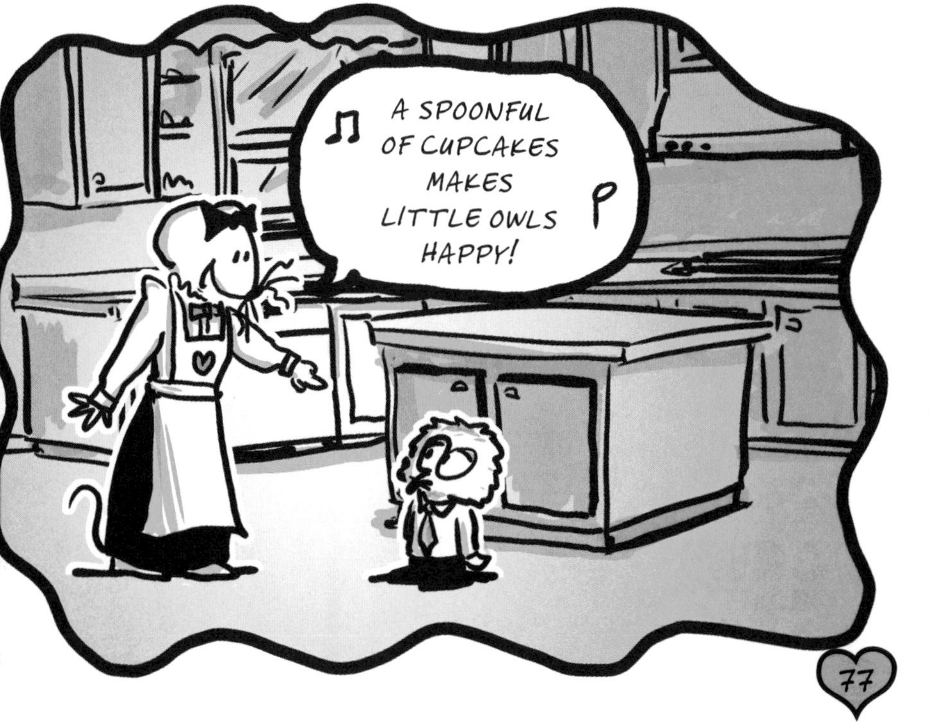
A SPOONFUL OF CUPCAKES MAKES LITTLE OWLS HAPPY!

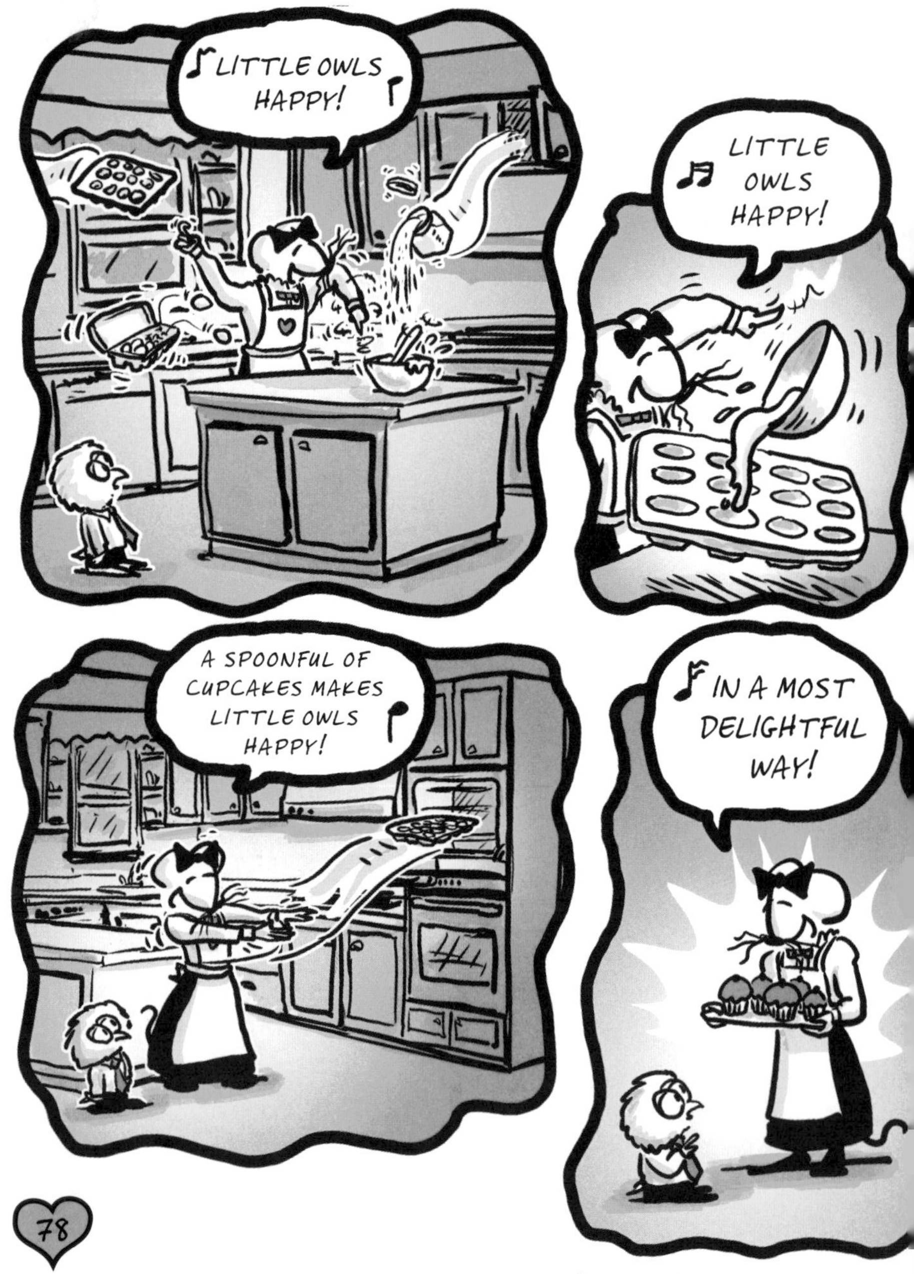
LITTLE OWLS HAPPY!
LITTLE OWLS HAPPY!
A SPOONFUL OF CUPCAKES MAKES LITTLE OWLS HAPPY!
IN A MOST DELIGHTFUL WAY!

SHAKE

SHAKE

I THINK YOU NEED MORE THAN A CUPCAKE TO CHEER THIS LITTLE GUY UP.

SIGH.

THE FOLLOWING WEEK.

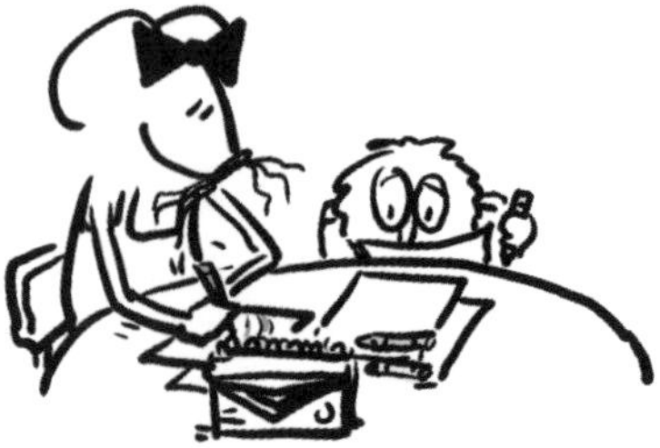

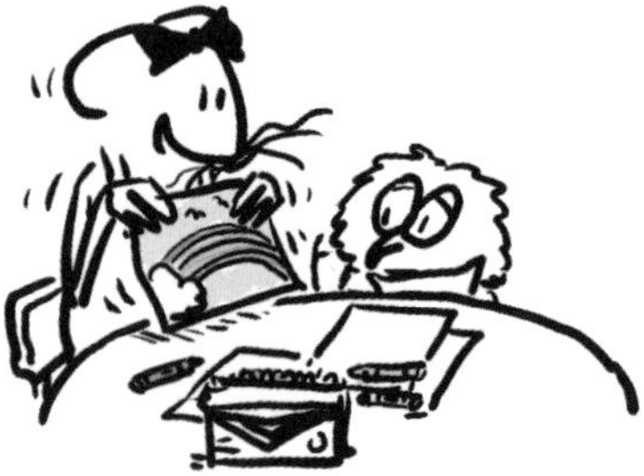

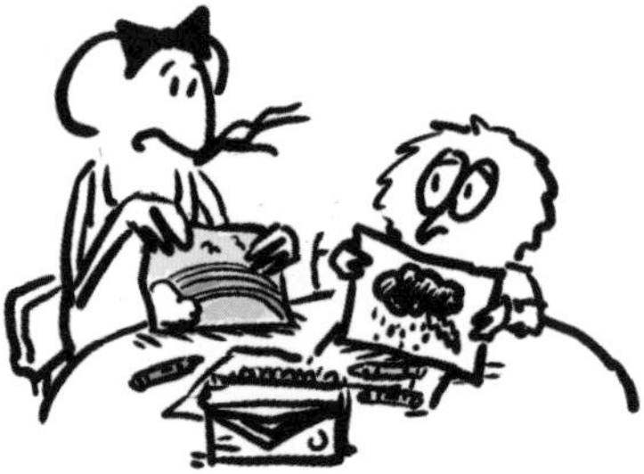

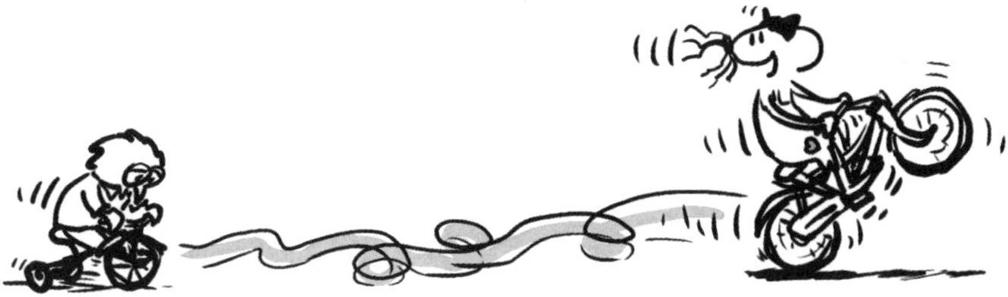

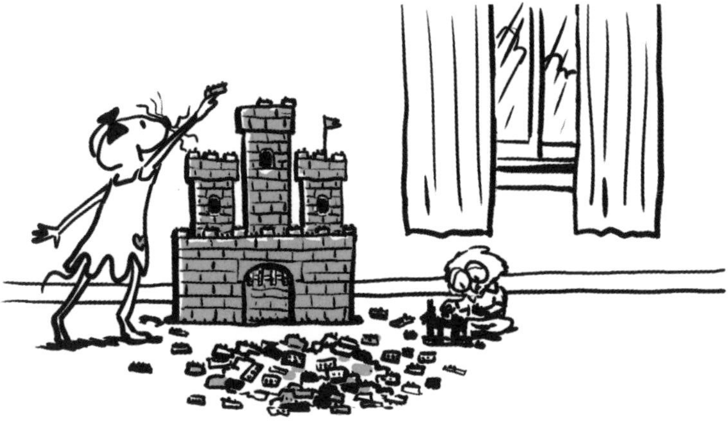

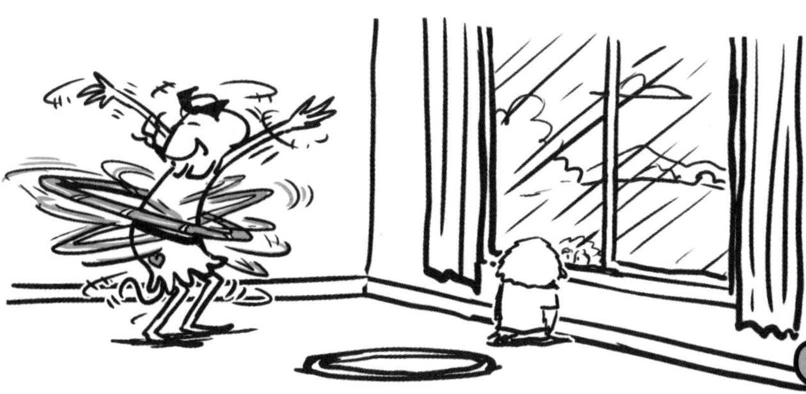

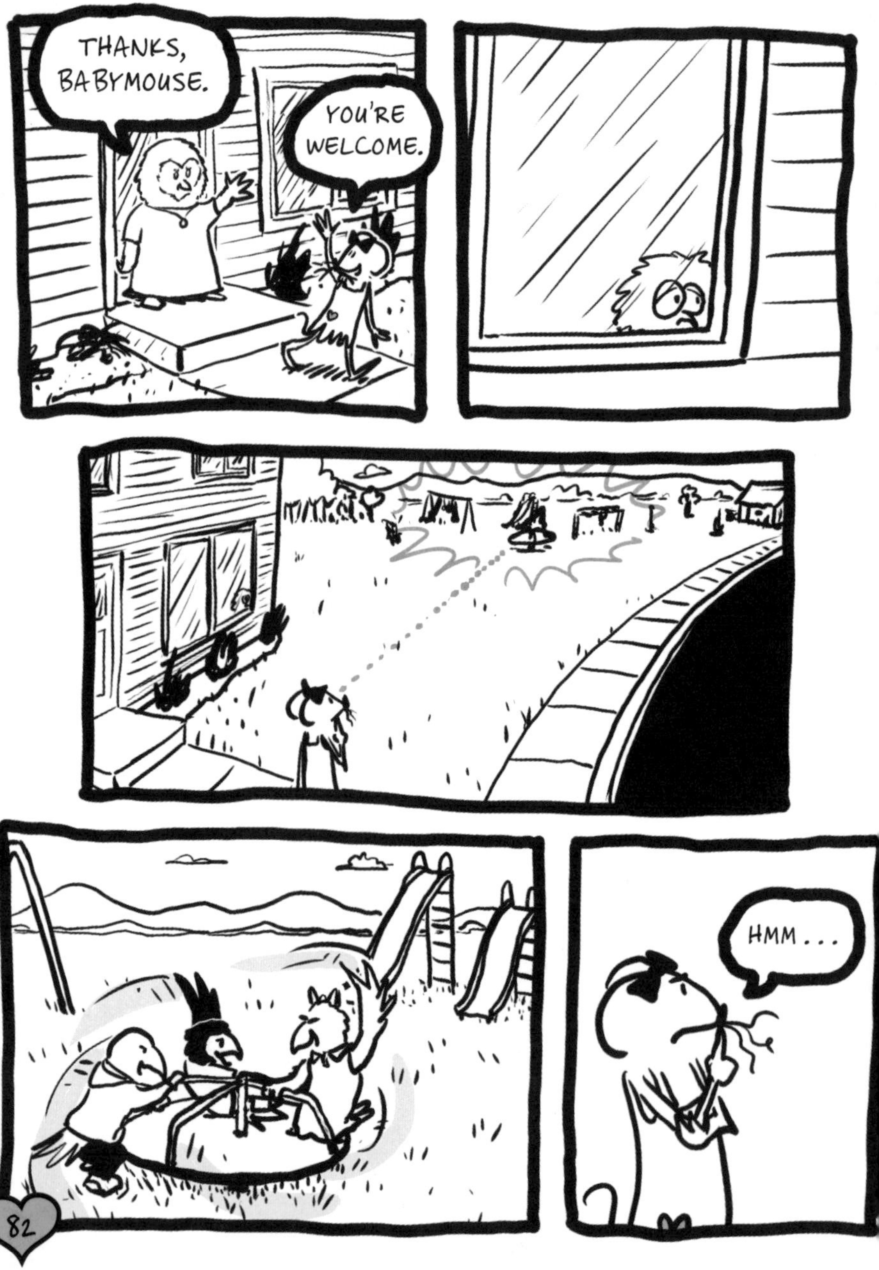
THANKS, BABYMOUSE.
YOU'RE WELCOME.
HMM . . .

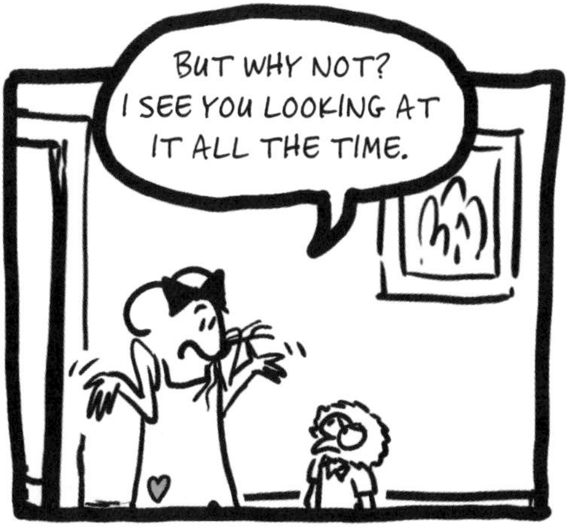

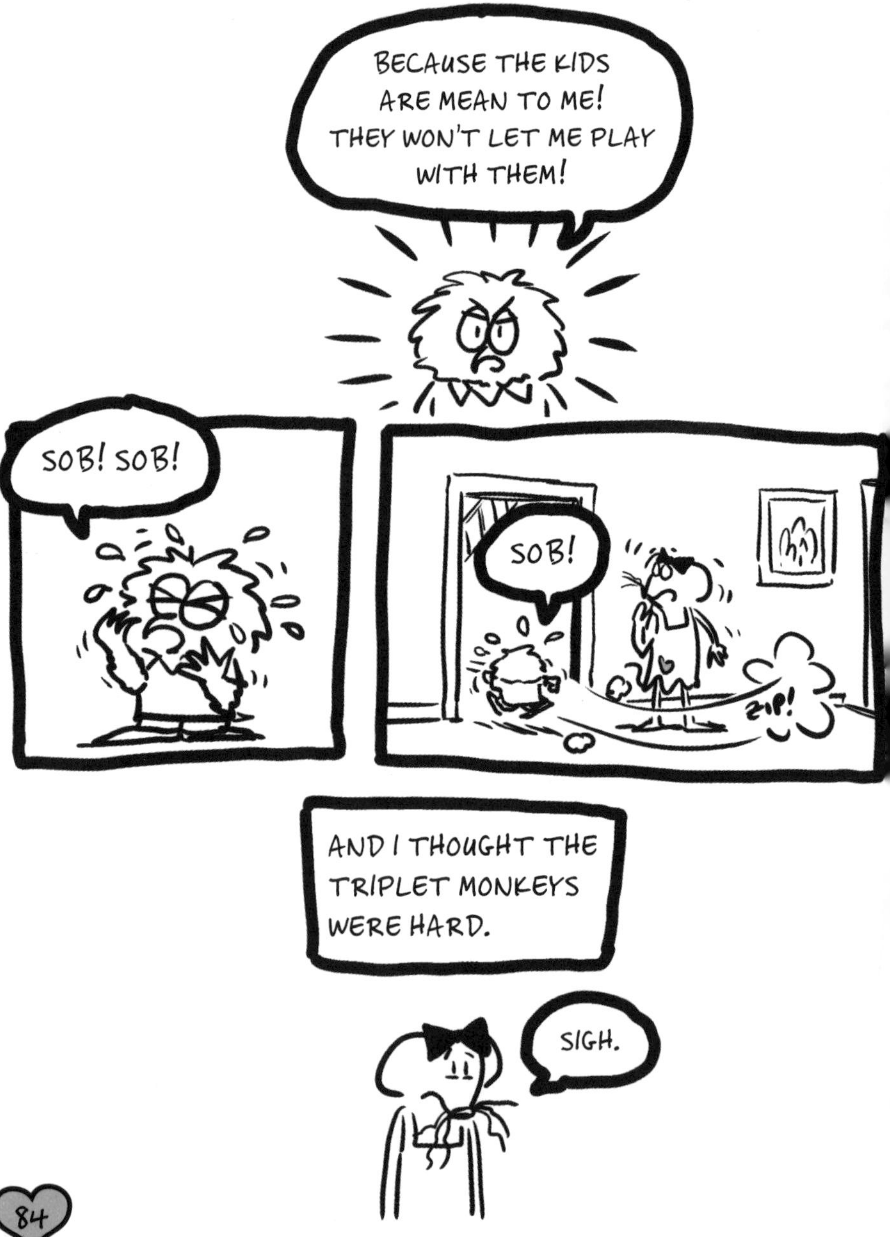

BECAUSE THE KIDS ARE MEAN TO ME! THEY WON'T LET ME PLAY WITH THEM!
SOB! SOB!
SOB!
ZIP!
AND I THOUGHT THE TRIPLET MONKEYS WERE HARD.
SIGH.

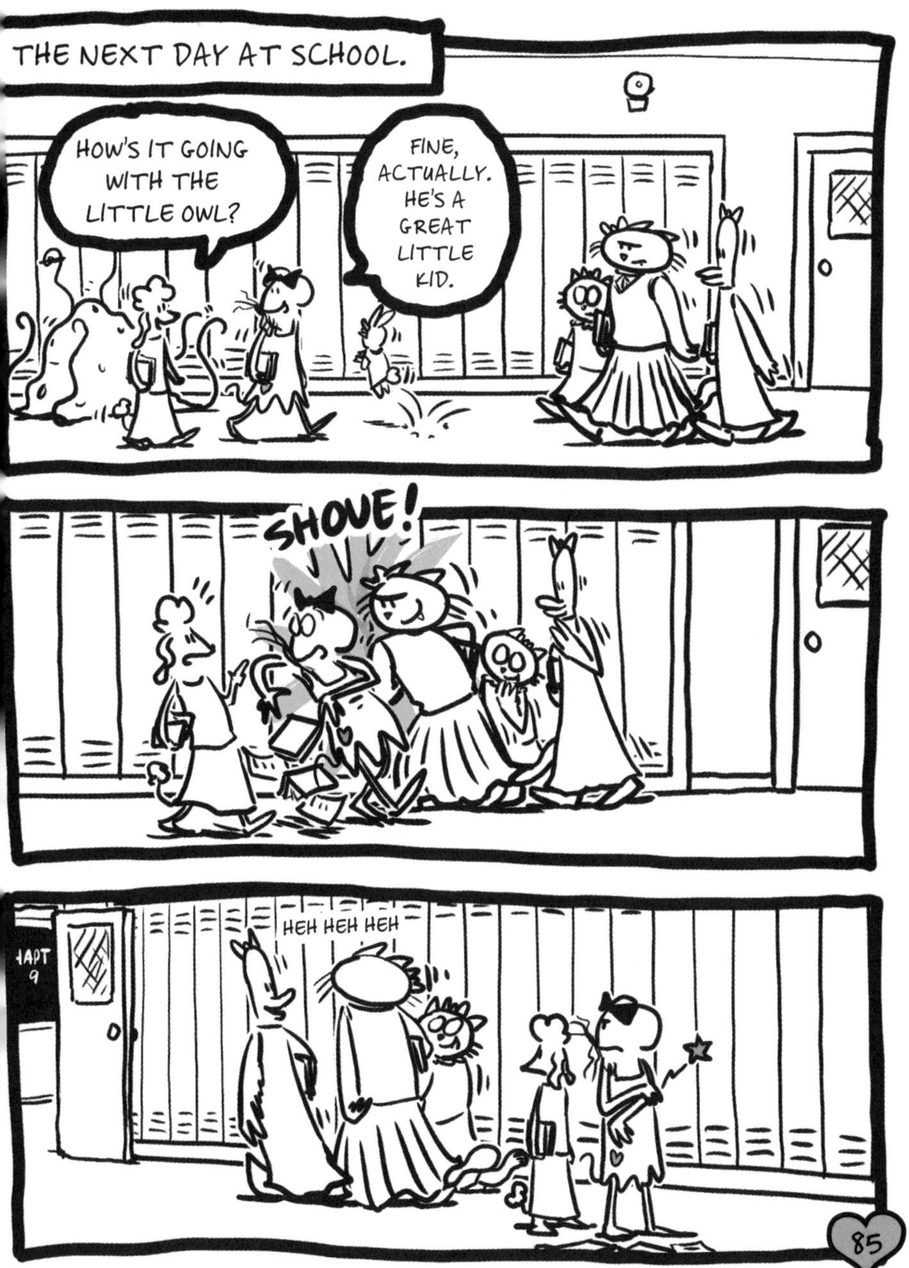
THE NEXT DAY AT SCHOOL.
HOW'S IT GOING WITH THE LITTLE OWL?
FINE, ACTUALLY. HE'S A GREAT LITTLE KID.
SHOVE!
HAPT 9
HEH HEH HEH

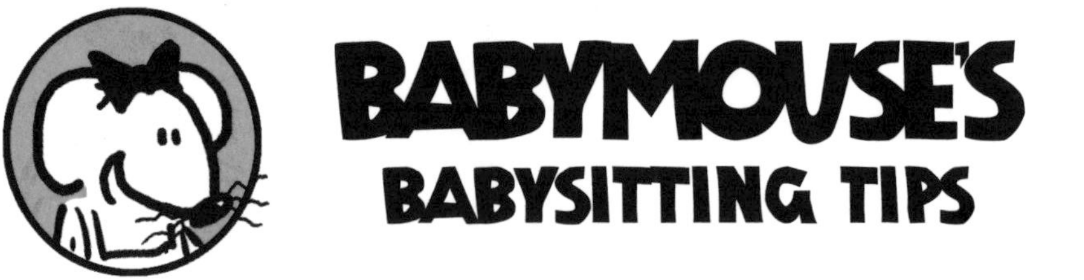

BABYMOUSE'S BABYSITTING TIPS

BE CHEERFUL!

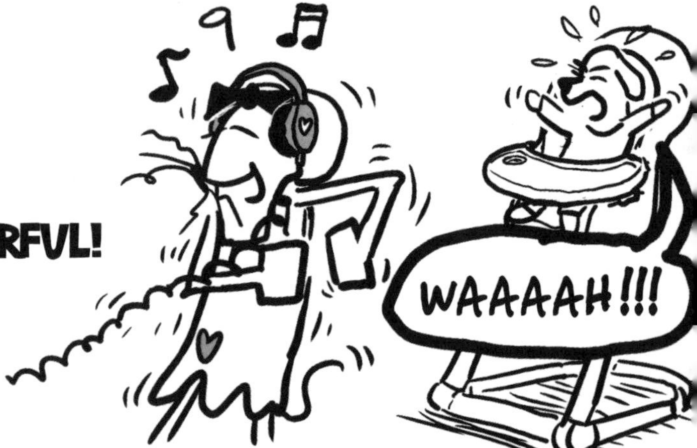
WAAAAH!!!

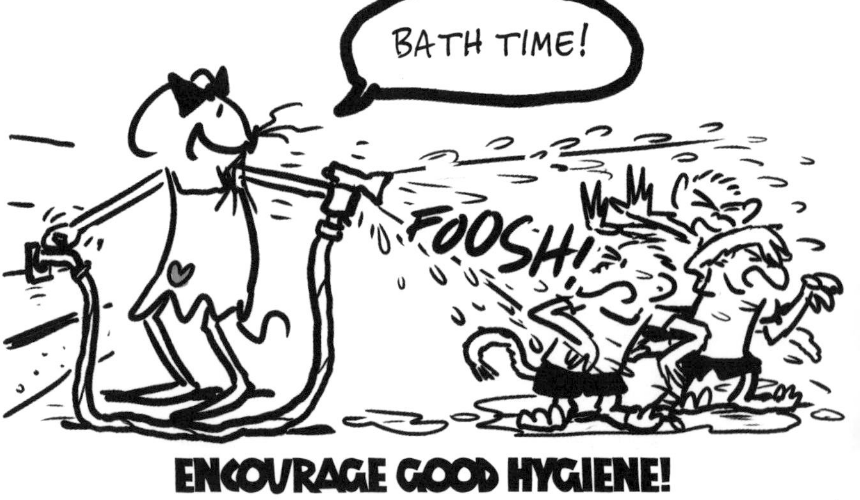
BATH TIME!
FOOSH!

ENCOURAGE GOOD HYGIENE!

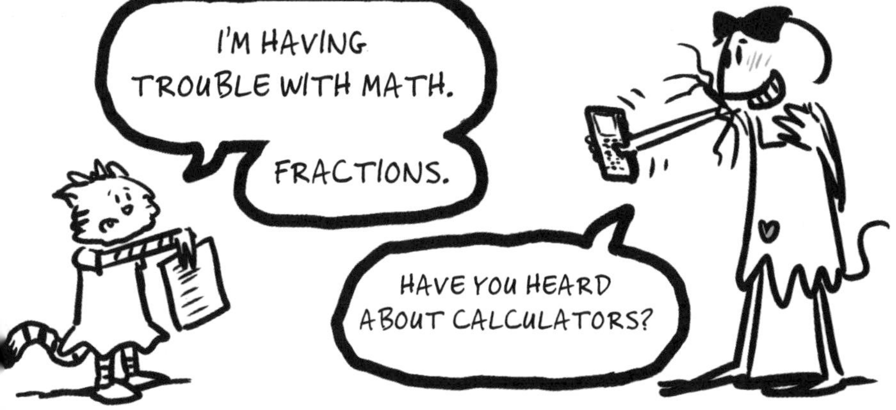
I'M HAVING TROUBLE WITH MATH.
FRACTIONS.
HAVE YOU HEARD ABOUT CALCULATORS?

HELP WITH HOMEWORK!

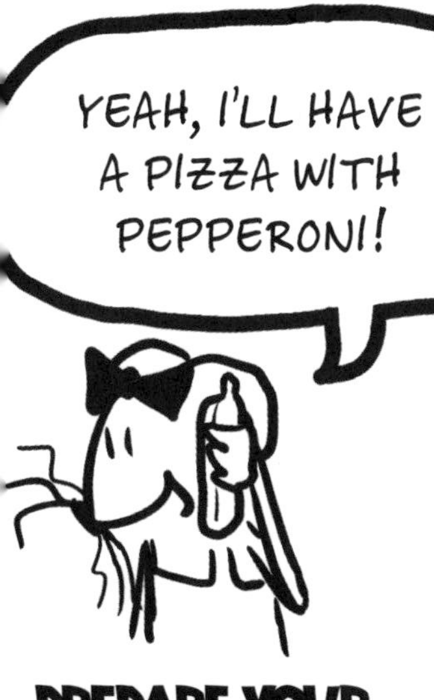
YEAH, I'LL HAVE A PIZZA WITH PEPPERONI!

PREPARE YOUR CHARGES A HEALTHY DINNER!

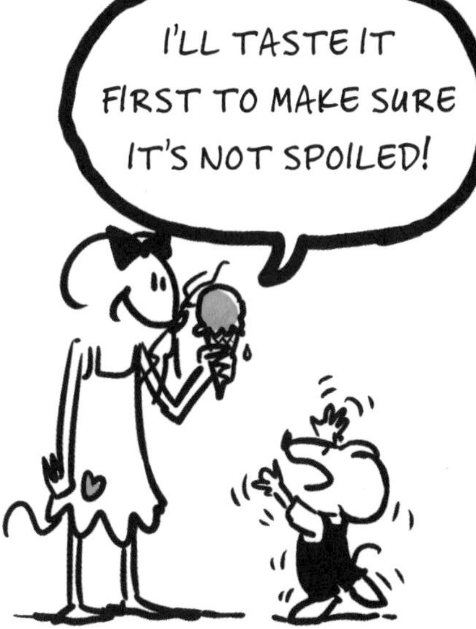
I'LL TASTE IT FIRST TO MAKE SURE IT'S NOT SPOILED!

ABOVE ALL, SAFETY FIRST!

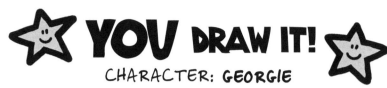

YOU DRAW IT!

CHARACTER: GEORGIE

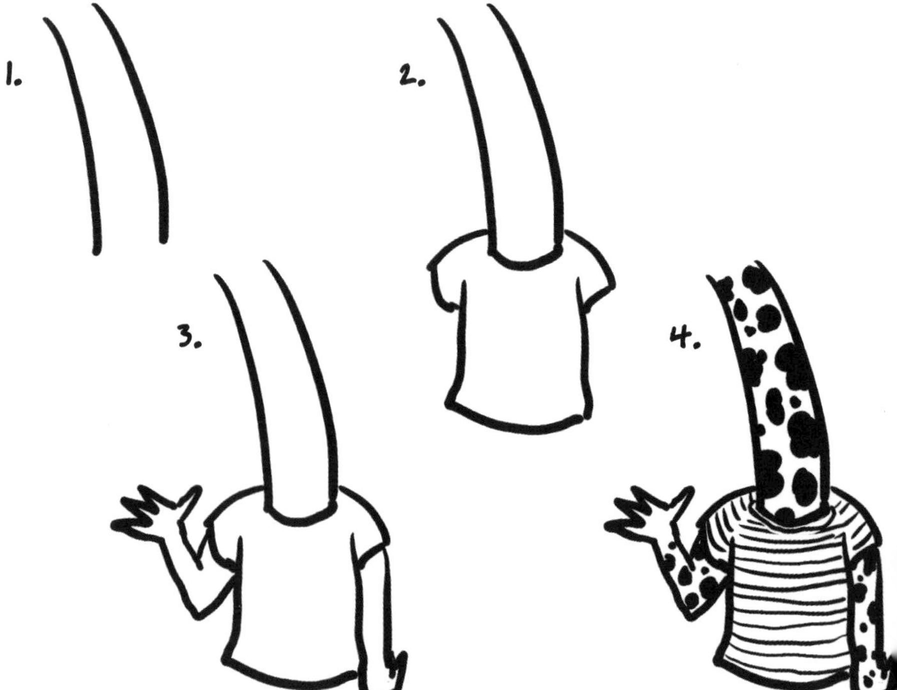
1.
2.
3.
4.

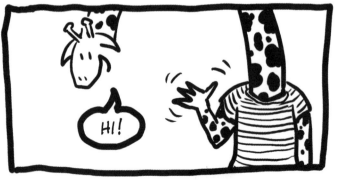

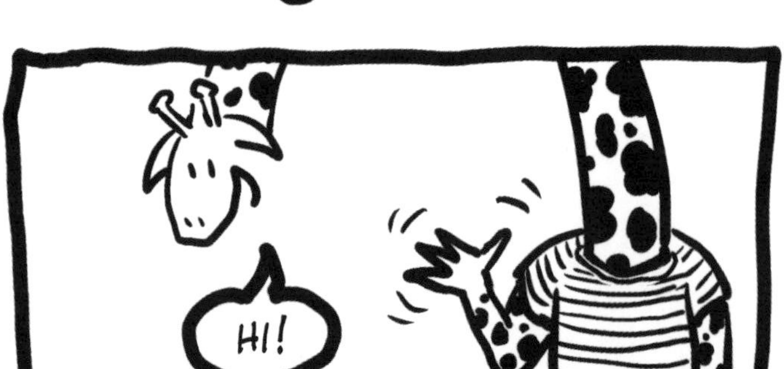
HI!

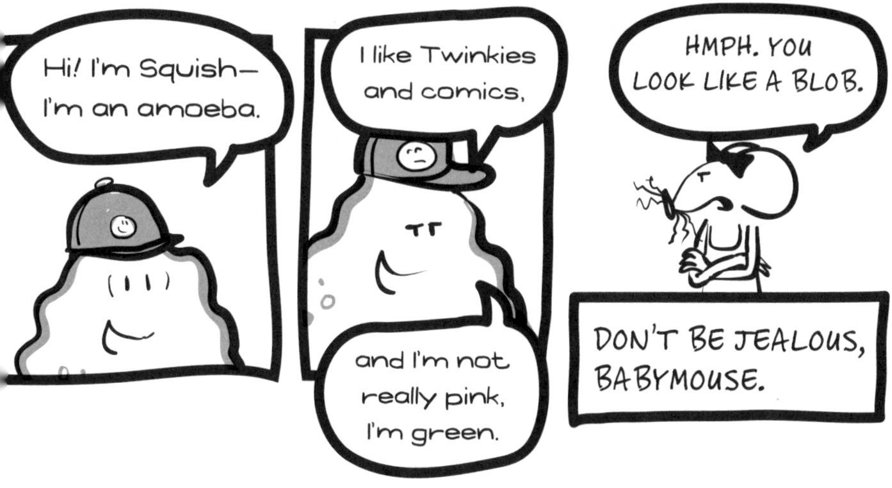
Hi! I'm Squish—
I'm an amoeba.
I like Twinkies
and comics,
and I'm not
really pink,
I'm green.
HMPH. YOU
LOOK LIKE A BLOB.
DON'T BE JEALOUS,
BABYMOUSE.

READ ABOUT
SQUISH'S AMAZING ADVENTURES IN:

#1 SQUISH: Super Amoeba

#2 SQUISH: Brave New Pond

#3 SQUISH: The Power of the Parasite

#4 SQUISH: Captain Disaster

#5 SQUISH: Game On!

#6 SQUISH: Fear the Amoeba

If you like Babymouse,
you'll love these other great books
by Jennifer L. Holm!

THE BOSTON JANE TRILOGY

EIGHTH GRADE IS MAKING ME SICK

THE FOURTEENTH GOLDFISH

MIDDLE SCHOOL IS WORSE THAN MEATLOAF

OUR ONLY MAY AMELIA

PENNY FROM HEAVEN

TURTLE IN PARADISE

THEY'RE REALLY GOOD! TRUST ME!